MW00760050

TALES, MYTHS & OTHER STORIES

Includes Adventures of the Superhero Mechanico Man

Dennis Nanni

Tony,
Let's get Crasy together!!
Hope you enjoy the Stories.

PublishAmerica
Baltimore

10/24/2012

© 2008 by Dennis Nanni.
All rights reserved. No part of this book may be reproduced, stored in a retrieval system or transmitted in any form or by any means without the prior written permission of the publishers, except by a reviewer who may quote brief passages in a review to be printed in a newspaper, magazine or journal.

First printing

All characters in this book are fictitious, and any resemblance to real persons, living or dead, is coincidental.

PublishAmerica has allowed this work to remain exactly as the author intended, verbatim, without editorial input.

Illustrations by Dennis Nanni

ISBN: 1-60610-837-9
PUBLISHED BY PUBLISHAMERICA, LLLP
www.publishamerica.com
Baltimore

Printed in the United States of America

It would seem to me the dedication might be the hardest part of writing a book; you sure don't want to leave anyone out. Special thanks to all the many friends, relatives, and loved ones, for they have tolerated a lot from me. To my father Joseph R. Nanni; he was a strict, dysfunctional, but very artistic man. I know he would have been pleased— may he rest in peace. Without his many stories, hundreds of hours playing music together, and his inspiration to be creative, this book may have never come to life.

I'd like to offer a very special dedication to my loving wife and best friend, Glenna, and the same to my son Dhanvantari. With the help of his imagination and through his home schooling, the foundations for these stories were laid. My mother-in-law, Maxine Brown, she is always there for us through thick and thin; Maxine thank you so much. To all the people mentioned above I love you all more than you can imagine.

Acknowledgments

It has taken me many years to compile this book, and I don't believe it would have made a difference without expert editorial help. When it comes to music I am somewhat complete in that I can play and I know the technical aspect. As far as writing, I can create and write it down (the playing part) as far as the technical (editing) I am somewhat lost. So I'd like to offer a grateful, warm, heart felt thanks to Dr. Michael Hartman, a dedicated English professor, who, along with English, teaches film at Motlow State College in Moore county Tennessee. Dr, Hartman has been teaching over 25 years. I met Dr. Hartman through my son who was in his class.

With the help of Dr. Hartman's experience and expertise, he has taken a piece of coal and polished it into a diamond. Thank you friend, I couldn't have done it without you.

Dennis 06/02/08

Table of Contents

Dark, Dark Days: a Witch Hunt

At the dawn of the Renaissance (the fifteenth century to sixteenth century), some developments began to coalesce into the "witch craze" that possessed Europe from about 1450 to 1700. During this period, thousands of people, mostly innocent women, were executed on the basis of "proofs" or "confessions" of diabolical witchcraft; here is such a story, only with a happy ending.

I write this story with vivid memories of what happened in those days; oh, those were dark, dark days. I am Ruth of Yorkshire. I was a young woman with a bright mind and independent ideas. I was always looking for something out of the ordinary. Then one particular day, believe me, I found it!

It was a sunny, warm day in May that year. I was about eleven years old. I was walking through the forest on the way to the village when I happened to observe a rather interesting looking older woman off the path. She was picking wild flowers and herbs, and gathering roots. She placed them carefully in her hand as if to sanctify them, then placed what she had gathered into a hand-woven covered basket. It seems she wanted to protect her precious find. Now, Mother told me never to speak to strangers while walking through the forest on my trip to the village. However, this woman seemed too kind and gentle to be a potential danger or threat; besides, I was curious about her activities.

"Hello," I said, "my name is Ruth of Yorkshire."

She looked up from her picking, smiled gently and replied, "Hello, my name is Gwen of Richwood."

"I was curious as to what you are doing with the plants you put into your beautiful basket."

"I will be glad to tell you. Would like to come to my cottage for tea and crumpets?"

Now I ask you, who can resist tea and crumpets? I had some time as I didn't have to be back from the village until supper. Mother always let me take my time walking through the market whenever I made the trip. Only this seemed like much more fun, so I answered yes. As we walked back to her home, I had many questions and inquiries. Gwen answered them expertly and excitedly as she was pleased that someone was interested in her work.

When we came upon the cottage it was in an opening in the forest; everything was simply breathtaking. The cottage was painted with vivid colors; it also had round top windows with flower boxes under each window.

Gwen of Richwood's cottage in the forest

Each box was filled with colorful flowers such as pansies, marigolds, calendula, and nasturtium. Lining the brick walkway were a mixture of zinnias and sunflowers; the lawn area was a rich green carpet broken up with perfectly-placed gardens of flowers, vegetables, and herbs. The inside was just as beautiful; each room was tastefully decorated with antiques and hand-painted furniture. Flowers from her gardens filled vases throughout; the fragrance was scintillating. There was also a variety of house plants that accented each room. Everything was clean, neat, and in place. We had our tea and crumpets and talked for some time, then said our goodbyes and off I went to the village.

From that very first meeting, we became very close and dear friends. Whenever I was not at school or doing chores, I was over Gwen's house, listening, learning, and taking in the wonderful aromas. Gwen was always brewing herbs for medicines or baking crumpets and bread sweets. When I asked her why she was doing this, she replied that she was helping the poor folks in the area who couldn't afford the market or the price of a doctor's visit in the village. As always when I visited, she was willing to show and teach me what she was doing. I absorbed the information like a dry sponge. Sometimes she let me travel with her to the homes of the folks she visited.

I did go to the village often and always enjoyed the trip; however, lately when I went there, it seemed there was a tension in the air that made me very uncomfortable. I would sometimes hear soft muffled talking amongst the townspeople, usually something about witches, witchcraft, and witch hunts. Although meeting Gwen was a bright spot at that time, these were, as I mentioned before, dark, dark days. People were very suspicious and fearful; anything unusual would usually lead to someone being arrested. Most of the time it would be women, especially if they were gifted or tried to be independent from the men they married; more times than not they were considered witches! This led to impromptu trials and unfair ludicrous sentencing such as burning at the stake or hanging by the neck. Even today when I think about those days it sends a chill down my spine.

I remember thinking about Gwen and her work, how it could be construed in the wrong way by those twisted, fearful townsfolk.

That particular day it felt good to get out of the village and back into the countryside; my whole body seemed to relax. On that day on the way back from the village, I decided to stop by Gwen's cottage.

Although I had never done this before, something inside told me to be cautious; maybe it was my young woman's intuition. I always cherished our visits and I didn't have anything that would spoil immediately so I thought it would be all right. It was a late, warm, humid afternoon in August; I was looking forward to a glass of cool mint tea that Gwen served in the warmer months. Walking through the woods right before the clearing, I paused and became very still. I heard a commotion with muffled angry voices. There was also the sound of a woman weeping. My heart stopped! Gwen's cottage was in that clearing! What could they possibly want with her?

It took me a minute but I figured what they wanted; it made me tremble. I hid behind a big maple tree waiting. Suddenly I heard a loud voice.

"Take this witch to the village—we shall have a trial right away!"

No, this couldn't be happening! I peeked around the tree; Gwen was lifted onto a horse, her hands and feet bound with rope, a kerchief tied around her mouth. I followed the men back to the village. Now the food might spoil and Mother would be worried, but what happened to my friend was very important. When they reached the village, preparations were already in progress in the village square for the mock trial. A large post was dug into the earth with straw and wood placed all around its base.

This can't be good; think, Ruth, think! Suddenly out of the courthouse an elderly man in a disheveled white wig and a soiled, wrinkled judge's robe appeared. He seemed to be both judge and prosecutor. He stood behind a makeshift table with a gavel in his hand he looked dazed as if almost intoxicated; I believe he probably was. How else could you send someone to her demise with such unfair swiftness? I had heard these trials were quick and to the point; sadly, I thought I was about to witness such a trial. After all, were not witches bad and evil; people wanted them gone!

The judge spoke without allowing Gwen to speak in her own defense. He addressed this hurriedly gathered crowd.

"Does anyone see why this Gwen of Richwood should not be tried, convicted, and burned at the stake as she is a witch?"

The sound of crowd was beginning to swell to a kind of hysteria! It was going to be hard for the judge to hear so I pushed my way to the front of the mob and yelled as loud as I could, "I do!"

Suddenly the hysteria calmed; it became as quiet as midnight.

"Speak up, little girl!" said the judge, half laughing, half amused. He continued, "What could a small child such as yourself have to say in defense of this evil woman?"

I walked to the center of the area where they had Gwen bound hand and foot with thick chains to the post as if she had some power to escape. Several armed guards stood around her; two of them had torches ready to light the fire when the sentence was handed down.

I gathered all my confidence and spoke with my best voice: "This person called Gwen of Richwood is not a witch; she is not evil, but just the opposite. I have been her close friend for two years and she has done nothing but good."

There was a curious stirring in the crowd. The judge seemed mildly interested.

"Continue," he said.

"I have seen her feed the poor, work selflessly to heal the sick. Some of you in this crowd have been her patients!"

I continued as best I could as her lone defendant: "She is not making secret potions or witches' brew, but herbal medicines to help the sick and the poor who could not afford to pay the doctor's fee. There is not a person here that Gwen of Richwood would not be willing to help, even if it meant giving the clothes off her own back!"

The face of the judge and the faces of the crowd softened and it became almost silent once more you could hear crickets chirping. The judge thought for a moment, then spoke.

"Maybe we have been too quick to judge this woman. It has been quite possible that some of the women we've tried as witches were indeed like Gwen of Richwood. The only difference is they didn't have anyone to defend them as this sweet young girl did for this woman. Release her! More of us should follow in the footsteps of Gwen of Richwood. As the judge for this village I vow from this time forward to execute my duties properly and set an example for judges in the surrounding towns and villages. The days of the mock witch trial is over; innocent people shall not perish!"

Gwen was unchained from the post; she ran over to me hugged and squeezed as hard as she could.

"You are my best friend! Thank you for believing in me; I will never forget you!"

I grabbed her arm and walked home with her in the full moonlight; neither of us spoke a word.

It was very late when I got home. Mother was very upset and worried; the supplies did indeed spoil, but when Mother found out what happened, she did not care. She was very proud of me and knew Gwen was my best friend and that I acted in her best interest. I'd like to think that in some small way I influenced the end of witch hunting. And yes, I still get together with Gwen to learn and assist, as I am now following in her footsteps. And as always, I savor the taste of her wonderful tea and crumpets; now I ask you, who can resist tea and crumpets?

The Tale of Gecko Mountain

Why do people like to be scared out of their wits; why must they have an external stimulus to frighten them when the world is scary enough? Don't know, you say? Well, maybe we can fix that. Anyway, it's just a tall tale; what do you think?

One day Clayton, Bismarck, and Noodles were bored. It was a warm spring evening, and they were looking for some fun.

"Hey guys let's go over to that new cave near farmer Mel's old peanut farm. You know they say anyone who goes in doesn't come out!"

Clayton was half thinking aloud during the last part of his statement.

"That's a bunch of hogwash!" Noodles replied. "Tain't nobody goes in there cause of the bats."

"You're just chicken, Noodles," retorted Clayton, detecting a little hesitation in Noodles' reply. Noodles got his name because of his blonde curly hair, not quite as curly as dreadlocks, but you know, like noodles.

Bismarck, who has been sitting quietly, finally

spoke out: "Instead of sittin' here arguing, let's go and see for ourselves; folks say lots of stuff, it is a new cave, so maybe we should check it out."

This may not have been a good move. The boys each bought bottled water and a rice cake (this is the twenty-first century, you know!) at the Quickie Mart and were on their way. They got in Clayton's four-wheel-drive pickup truck and started on their way to the cave. Clayton had just gotten his license a few weeks back and was anxious to drive his new truck, and this seemed to be the perfect excuse. As was mentioned before, this may not have been the brightest of ideas. It was about a one hour drive to the old peanut farm and another twenty minutes on foot to the cave; that's if the old path wasn't grown over. There were two machetes behind Clayton's seat, so if they had to slash their way to the cave, they could.

"Wish I had bought a bag of chips instead of this!" Bismarck complained of his rice cake.

"Don't fret none, we'll be home in time for a late night stop at the Dairy Queen!" replied Noodles, now slightly less confident than before they started.

Naturally by the time they parked the truck, the sun was sinking below the horizon as ominous storm clouds began to roll in from the south.

"The path's all grown over! We're going to have to cut our way to the cave!" Clayton shouted as he walked back towards the truck to retrieve the machetes. Clayton and Bismarck both took the machetes and began slashing, Noodles followed reluctantly but closely behind. After what seemed like hours, but was probably about forty-five minutes due to all the slashing, they finally reached the cave entrance. It now was almost completely dark; they had no flashlight, only a cigarette lighter Bismarck purchased at the Quickie Mart.

"Good thinking, Bismarck," was the reply Clayton made when they discovered two oil-soaked torches just outside of the entrance of the cave.

"What are these doing here?" Noodles asked nervously.

"Who knows?" replied Clayton, "If we're going to find out what's inside this cave we'll have use them. You really are *chicken,* Noodles. Hey, 'Chicken Noodles,' get it?"

Noodles, Clayton, and Bismarck enter the cave

At that moment, thunder rumbled and the air became chilled. They lit the torches and started into the depths of the cave: Noodles observed that there were no bats. He wished he'd waited in the truck; better yet, he began to wish he hadn't come at all. This new cave was unlike any other cave; it wasn't damp, dank, and musty as are most caves. Instead, it was a bit warm and somewhat sweet-smelling. Outside the cave, it was now thundering madly and it sounded as if the wind were blowing very hard. They had walked for about a hundred yards when they thought they heard something in front of them. They stopped in their tracks and didn't make a sound; in fact, they almost stopped breathing. The sound was a very unusual sort of like a clanking or rattling. Naturally that type of sound that will make almost anyone think of, well, you know—spirits of the not-so-friendly kind.

Clayton yelled, his voice quivering, "I told you this cave is haunted! Now maybe you guys will believe me!"

Noodles and Bismarck were too frightened to speak; they looked at Clayton in agreement. The boys were too far in the cave to turn back, or so it seemed as they could no longer see the cave entrance. They moved forward cautiously hanging on to each other like little children.

Suddenly they heard a whooshing sound off to the right; a cool breeze started to blow. This actually was a relief, with the cave being warm and the three of them sweating from fright. Finally Noodles tried to speak.

"May-may-maybe we shouldn't be scared. How do we know this is a bad or evil situation?" The floor of the cave started to shake and there was a rumbling noise. Barely able to remain standing, they clung to each other like they were glued together.

"HELP!" they cried.

"We're all going to die! I'm too young!" shouted Bismarck.

The cave began to rumble more and more; suddenly they realized this didn't seem like a cave but something else. But what, what could it be? A thick oozing liquid started flowing into the cave and around their feet. It startled Noodles, who was carrying one of the torches; he dropped it into the ooze and it was immediately dissolved—nothing was left. They instantly climbed to higher ground but the rocks did not feel solid. The higher they climbed, the higher the thick mysterious ooze rose. With the rumbling and the ooze, it seemed a visit to Dairy Queen would have to wait.

When their heads almost touched the cave's ceiling, Clayton realized something he had observed at the entrance to the cave; the rocks were very jagged, almost like teeth, and the first twenty or so feet of the cave floor was soft and spongy. What about the warm sweet smell? No other cave is like this. Looking at each other they realized this wasn't a cave, it was ...... the ooze reached the ceiling.

The next morning, old farmer Mel found Clayton's four-wheeler with the keys sitting on the front seat.

"I might as well drive this over to the house jest in case they show up a-lookin' fer it."

After several hours of waiting Farmer Mel realized the boys were missing! Farmer Mel called his old friend Chief Peabody and Jed at the town barber shop, telling them the news.

Back in town the news spread quickly. For some time now, there had been talk about a newly-formed hillside that contained a cave. A group of men at Jed's Barber Shop were talking; one of them was a geologist. His name was Louis.

"Usually when a mountain or hilly area is formed, it's from an earthquake where the earth's tectonic plates shift and heave up or downward.

One of the other men chimed in, "Or from one of them there volcanoes!"

"That's correct; usually it take thousands of years!" Louis exclaimed.

Harlan Crimp, the town's mayor was also present, he said, "Seems to me somethin's wrong. How could a hillside with a cave just appear and those boys just disappear? I think we need to round up the townspeople, form a caravan, and take a ride out to that new cave."

"Yeh, let's go!" the men shouted in unison.

Mayor Crimp phoned farmer Mel and told him of their plans: "Come on up with the fellas. I've been wonderin' 'bout that cave myself, don't remember it bein' here before. I'll have some cool sassperilly waitin' fer ya. Although from the looks of things, ya might be needin' somethin' a little stronger than sassperilly!"

In about an hour, four pickup trucks were lined in front of Jed's Barber shop. Jed closed his shop early so he could join in on this mysterious search. One of the trucks was full of ladies as they wanted to help in the search. As they were about to pull away, a Jeep joined what was now the small caravan. It was Police Chief Peabody.

"Howdy, men, ladies, farmer Mel phoned me also. I guess you know the three boys that went up to the new cave haven't returned; I'm figurin' they might be in some kind of trouble. You folks might need some legal help; besides you will need my badge in case we have to resort to firepower."

"Always glad to have you along," replied the mayor. "All right, folks, let's move out!"

Chief Peabody assumed the head of the caravan and off they drove to farmer Mel's. There was so much anxiety and excitement in the group that you could feel the energy. Close to an hour later they arrived at farmer Mel's door.

"Come on in fer a spell! I got somethin' to tell ya!" Mel seemed very excited.

They all filed into farmer Mel's huge kitchen and all found a spot to settle in.

"Quite a bunch ya got here, mayor. I see even Peabody decided to tag along."

Before anyone could say anything Mel continued, "The cave has moved!"

Every single mouth in that kitchen dropped open, almost to the floor. Everyone now knew there was definitely something askew. Two of the ladies and the town diner owner Phil set up shop in the kitchen.

"I'm just not the adventurous type; they told me they needed my truck for supplies," said Phil. The rest of the group gathered all the supplies and gear they'd need and told the kitchen crew they would keep in touch with them by their cell phone. As they walked out the door, farmer Mel grabbed his shot gun.

They followed the path the boys had chopped through the brush to where the cave should have been. When they got there, they discovered some peculiar markings in the dirt. Everyone was puzzled; finally Zeke Clayborn, Clayton's father, also a local tour guide and animal tracker, spoke.

"These here markings look like snake scales giant, snake scales!" Suddenly the ground under their feet began to rumble and shake; several in the group lost their balance and had to grab onto one another to stay upright.

"What in tarnation was that?" stammered farmer Mel.

Louis spoke up: "Apparently we've had a small earthquake or... Zeke's giant snake is on the move."

Louis had brought a portable seismograph along and was able to locate where the epicenter of the rumble originated: "Come on, the disturbance originated near Critter Creek!"

The creek received its name because it attracted many kinds of wildlife. As everyone started to move, you could hear the sound of guns being loaded and triggers cocked.

"No shooting unless I say so; we don't need anybody hurt! Put the safeties on your guns!"

shouted Chief Peabody. Everyone moved quietly and cautiously with Louis at the front along side Chief Peabody. They would all have to walk about a half mile more before reaching the creek. Finally the only woman with them broke the silence; her name was Mandie Gold, a robust, tomboyish type, yet very attractive. She always kept a chaw of tobacco in the front of her mouth.

"You know, fellas, in this situation, don't you think maybe we should split into two groups?" She spat to the side and continued, "After all, there's a dozen of us here it might be better if we approached from two sides."

Chief Peabody broke in: "We might want to do that later but not just yet; we should see what we're up against first. Mandie, what did I tell you about chewin' that stuff?"

"I know, Chief, but I'm so nervous and excited I can't help chewin',"" she answered. The Chief just smiled and waved his arm for everyone to keep moving.

They hadn't walked one hundred steps when they froze in their tracks as the ground trembled slightly.

"Still comin' from the creek!" Louis shouted. They all started walking again, everyone craning their necks, glancing up and down the countryside which had now become slightly hilly. They were looking for something unusual or unfamiliar which at this point wasn't real difficult. The group walked uninterrupted for about ten minutes when they began to here the rushing waters of the Critter Creek.

"Everyone keep a sharp eye and be careful!" ordered the police chief.

Farmer Mel, who knew the lay of the land better than anyone, was now slightly ahead of the group.

Chief Peabody instructs the group, farmer Mel listens

"Hey I don't recognize them two hills over there, they wasn't here yesterday!" he said.

Chief Peabody spoke up, "Now let's do what Mandie said, split up into two groups of six. Mandie you can lead the second group. Louis, Mel, you're with me." At this point Chief Peabody handed

Mandie a headphone set. "Mandie, hook that up to your phone; you just have to push send and you'll connect directly to me. Listen for my call also—we don't know what we're going to run into and it could get noisy. You and your group approach from the western side; we'll approach from the east."

"Yes sir, Chief!" She was so excited that she swallowed her chaw. A kind of pale green color came over her twisted face. "I'll be fine, don't worry; it's not the first time I've done that!"

"All right now, everyone be quiet; the only communication will be hand signals, and if we get out of sight, through the head set. Squad two follow the instructions of your leader; she's getting her orders directly from me!"

As the chief spoke, it began to sound like a military exercise. Slowly the two squads began to approach the two hills from either side. Nothing seemed that unusual except for the same sweet smell the boys had experienced.

When Mandie's group came around from their side they came smack in front of the cave entrance. Mandy pushed "send"; the chief answered immediately.

"Chief here; what's up?"

"I'm in front of the cave entrance or whatever it is," Mandie whispered.

"Stay right there; don't move. Wait for us to come around—we'll be there in a couple of minutes." The chief and his squad hurried to meet Mandie's squad.

The wait seemed like hours instead of minutes; finally the chief's squad approached.

"You guys all right?" Louis asked.

"We're fine," Zeke Clayborn responded; he was in Mandie's squad.

"Before we go any further somethin's been a-gnawin' at me, Zeke. You named your son Clayton Clayborn?" farmer Mel asked.

"That's right; Clayton C. Clayborn, to be exact. C stands for Cactus."

"All right, that's enough chit-chat; we have to get serious here!" Mayor Crimp finally spoke out. He'd been silent for most of the trip and was also in Mandie's squad.

"As we all know, once the boys went in, they didn't come out. We have to have a plan; we don't want to lose anyone else. Any ideas, anyone?"

For the next few minutes no one spoke; it was like twelve minds were trying to come up with a perfect, flawless, safe, solution. However, it was not to be. All at once a huge wind came from inside the cave; it didn't blow them away, and instead it sucked them inside! It happened so fast no one knew what hit them; now they were inside on the same spongy floor as the boys.

"We can't let what happened to the boys happen to us!" Louis was talking as he tried to get his seismograph working. Luckily the batteries still had a charge in them, but to no avail.

"This is not mineral, as we know, and since we came inside the instrument will not function. The sweet smell we noticed outside the cave is much stronger in here and look at these jagged tooth-shaped formations. Besides, what happened to the entrance to the cave?" Louis was trying not to panic as he spoke. When the strange wind sucked them inside it also brought in all of the supplies. Nobody noticed that five sticks of dynamite and pouch of gun powder broke loose from the supply pack and were lying about twenty or thirty feet away from them further into the cave. Mandie looked up and thought she saw small openings about twenty feet above the jagged rocks. She poked Chief Peabody.

"Maybe there's a way out," she said, as she pointed upward. Upon hearing Mandie, everyone gathered around and looked up to see the possible escape route.

Zeke Clayborn broke the silence. "What about finding the boys—shouldn't we look before trying to get out?"

Voices from the remaining eleven of them shouted in agreement, "Yes!"

"Let's go find them!" yelled someone from the crowd.

"Everyone simmer down!" shouted the mayor, "I agree we should look for the boys."

Chief Peabody added, "Here's the plan; we'll head into the cave single file. Two of you will remain here with the headset. Since you already have the headset on, Mandie, you'll be one of them." Mandie started to protest but realized once the chief made a decision it would stand.

"Jed, I want you to stay with her. If something should happen, you know everyone in town, so you'll be able to keep things going. I'm going to tie a rope around one of these jagged rocks; I'll unravel the rope as we proceed into the depths of the cave. It's really dark in here; Zeke, light a match and look in the supplies for the flash lights."

Zeke did as the chief, requested found the flashlights, and threw the match to the ground. Remember what fell out of the supply pack? No sooner did the match hit the ground than the gun powder ignited. Everyone panicked and ran toward the front of the cave right under the openings Mandie had discovered.

"She's gonna blow!" screamed farmer Mel. With a deafening blast, the dynamite exploded, the ground shook, and the front part of the cave disintegrated. It was so loud they heard the blast back in town. Soon coughing and light cries broke the eerie silence that followed the blast.

Mayor Crimp was the first to speak up: "Is everyone O.K.? Call out, let me hear your names."

"Mel, Louis, Mandie, Zeke." One by one the twelve called out; everyone survived! Aside from a few minor scrapes and bruises, everyone was fine. What made the incident even more mysterious is the twelve of them landed about fifty yards from the cave entrance.

"How's this possible?" Farmer Mel seemed to be talking as if in shock or dazed and to no one in particular.

"Once the dust settles we're going to go back and find out how we're still alive!" Louis answered while dusting himself off. In the meantime, farmer Mel called back to the farm house to see how the ladies and Phil were doing.

"This here is Mel callin', how's it goin' back there?"

Phil answered the phone, "We're fine; what was that loud noise? It shook the whole house."

"There's been an explosion; we'll probably be here till dark."

"Great—there goes my Shrimp Scampi." Phil sounded depressed.

"Sorry, Phil we kinda have an emergency here." Farmer Mel said goodbye and closed his phone.

The dust finally did settle; the twelve of them were calmed down, bruises and scrapes were cared for, everyone had a rice cake and water (this is the twenty-first century, you know).

"Yuk, don't reckon I'll ever get used to those new fangled what-cha-ma-call-em cakes," said Farmer Mel. Finally after much conversation, they cautiously and curiously headed back towards the cave entrance.

"No need to split up now; seems it'd be better if we stayed together," said the chief. When they got to the cave, their eyes just about popped out of their heads! For a moment they stood there in awe; it wasn't a cave, or a mountain, in fact, not even a snake. It was a lizard, a giant lizard.

"You were pretty near right, Zeke," said Farmer Mel. Everyone else shook their heads in agreement. The explosion had singed the lizard so he was perfectly preserved. Due to its unusual color, the lizard blended perfectly with the landscape.

"I guess there's not much else we can do here;

we'll have to come back in the morning to look for the boys. By the time we get back to Mel's house, it will be dark."

Mandie spoke up, "Do you hear something? Sounds like voices, muffled voices in the distance." Everyone was quiet; they perked their ears toward the sound; the voices became clearer and closer.

"Hey everybody it's us, Clayton, Bismarck, and Noodles!" Now three distant figures were running towards them. All the fathers of the boys were in the group and when they saw the boys, they began running towards them. Tears were running down the boys' faces, their fathers' faces, oh what the hey, pretty soon everyone was in tears! It was kind of weird, for along with the tears, everyone was jumpin' and hootin' and hollerin' as Farmer Mel would say. Everyone gathered around the boys and things calmed down.

Chief Peabody asked, "What happened to you fellas? Were you in the lizard cave, and if so how did you escape?" Clayton and the other boys were so elated to see everyone they could hardly speak.

Noodles began, "Yes, we were in the lizard, only at the time we didn't know it was a lizard; we really thought it was a cave."

Bismarck continued, "As we went deeper into the cave, it kinda became clear something was wrong, you know, the sweet smell and spongy floor."

"Then the thick oozy stuff started to swallow us up; we ran toward the top of the cave and then came what sounded like a giant sneeze! We were thrust out of the cave. We've been groggy, lost ever since. Then we heard the explosion and your voices and started running towards the sound," added Clayton.

"Let's head back to my place; Phil's cookin' up some skip shrimpy or somethin'," suggested Farmer Mel. "I got runnin' water too, so you can all clean up!"

Before you could say "let's go," everybody was walking back towards Farmer Mel's house talking excitedly about the last couple of days' adventure. They were all hungry and happy even though all of them had an unbelievable experience with a giant lizard that doubled as a cave.

A few days later a local scientist, Louis the geologist, and the state environmentalist, went out to study the giant preserved lizard. After much study, an analysis seemed that this was nothing more than a common Gecko lizard that had somehow gotten into some nuclear waste from the nearby deserted nuclear plant and mutated into a giant (seems like these folks have an extremely more serious problem!).

How the twelve rescuers were saved goes like this. When the gunpowder started burning, it made the lizard's tongue hot; he rolled up his tongue to spit out the fire. When the dynamite exploded, the twelve were thrown out of the lizard's month in his rolled up tongue, therefore saved from the explosion and basically unharmed. The lizard would be forever preserved at the creek due to the mutation and the explosion.

"I hope he wasn't in town to do an insurance commercial," chuckled Noodles, "we ain't got cars that big."

So if you ever ride by an old peanut farm and see a sign, "Preserved Lizard Preserve," stop in and see Farmer Mel; he might just give you a free tour. Oh, and by the way, if you're in town, directions to his farm are right next to the Dairy Queen.

The Legend & Adventures of Mechanico Man

Tim 'Speed" Boatman was fanatical and eccentric when it came to fast speedboats; otherwise, he was an ordinary fellow. What happens to Tim in this saga is the beginning and unfolding of a very unusual, unbelievably fantastic superhero that is far from ordinary.

Chapter #1

Once upon a time (what, you want something different?), there was a boat mechanic who lived on the shore of a peaceful lake in Tennessee not so long ago. Tim "Speed" Boatman was known by everyone in the area, a likeable, friendly man who would help anyone who needed the assistance. In fact, there were times you didn't have to ask; Tim was there for you. He had his boat repair shop on the dock located at the north end of the lake.

Tim was always busy. He was perceived as a little odd for his obsession to make faster and faster speed boats, dangerously fast boats. In fact, his boats were so fast that he ingeniously fabricated a uniform out of strips of aluminum. This was to protect him from flying objects caused from going at such a high speed; sometimes those objects were actually the parts from his boat. Thus, he lovingly received the name Mechanico Man because of how he looked when wearing his protective uniform. He actually liked the name and soon that was how he was known throughout the area. If you wanted your boat or boat engine repaired first class, "Go out to the lake and see "Mechanico Man."

Mechanico Man was also a techno-science aficionado; he always read *Modern Science* magazine and had every technical catalog available. So any kind of advancement in electronics that he could use in his boats and engines he learned and put to use. He also used this technology in his customer's repairs whenever he could. When trying to build one of his own speed boats he would use motors and engines from every type of machine he could find. Mechanico Man would then modify his engines with gadgets and technology.

Now during those days, the lake was a quiet and peaceful place. Cottages lined the north end of the lake where Tim Boatman and other families lived. This lake is still there today, a great place for fishing, boating, and relaxing, although it has undergone some amazing changes that you will find out in this story.

Usually the only time there was a disruption was when Tim tested one of his engines or boats. The neighbors in the surrounding area were used to Tim's testing, and being a good neighbor, he tried to keep his testing to minimum. However, there was this one particular time when he tried installing an engine from and old blimp on his latest boat. And what a boat this was; it was sleek, aerodynamic, and had a hull made from titanium. The titanium came from a scrapped experimental plane from the local air force base. It seems he had gotten a Ford-built engine from an old World War I survey blimp. He found the engine in an old barn of a friend of his mother's uncle on a farm in the hills of southern Tennessee.

This engine was very powerful; his mother's uncle said it was close to eight hundred horsepower. Along with the engine came a giant ten foot propeller from that same blimp. Tim hoped that engine and propeller would hurl him across the lake faster than anything he had ever tried. When the neighbors heard of his latest venture, they just shook their heads in disbelief.

"He's really done it this time," was the general consensus.

There had been talk in the nearby town that the electric company was going to extend the lake and build a dam to harness the lake's power for electricity in the now-growing communities in the area. They had selected several locations along the lake but had not made a final decision as to where the dam would be. Meanwhile, Tim "Speed" Boatman continued working on his now all-time fastest speedboat. Along the lake at that time there was the Acme concrete plant; they manufactured concrete for all types of construction in the immediate area. The only thing that interfered with this beautiful lake scenery was the mounds of sand, rock, and lime that went into the making of the concrete. When the time came for the dam actually to be built, the concrete plant was going to be dismantled and moved closer to the town and its growing population. The lake would then have flawless beauty throughout as the dam was designed to blend in with the lake and the lakeside landscape.

Finally, the day came when Tim "Speed" Boatman, alias Mechanico Man's, feat of engineering was ready to try, or should we say, fly? The name of this boat was "Masterpiece One." Now this was some kind of boat, an amazing piece of machinery with every gadget and doodad available; it even had a device installed called a cassette player. The cassette player was a tape machine for listening to music, why Mechanico Man thought he'd be able to listen to music during this test is a mystery.

"Just part of his crazy eccentric ways," said his wife Abigail. Also on board was a radio transceiver so he could communicate with a home base which would be his residence. His wife Abigail would operate the transceiver at the house. He decided to test the boat early on a Sunday morning when everyone was at home, lucky for everyone that he did. He woke up about four a.m., put on his newly-designed double thick Mechanico Man uniform, kissed his wife; she sleepily opened her eyes, kissed him back, and wished him luck. At that moment she turned on her transceiver to be able to communicate with her loving husband.

Upon seeing the lights flashing and dials glowing on Abigail's transceiver, off he went to the dock to start on his trek to pilot what he hoped would be the world's fastest speedboat.

"I'll make the record books," he thought.

When he got to his dock where Masterpiece One was moored, the sun was just starting to rise over the lake's placid water. Mechanico Man knew this test was extremely dangerous though he wouldn't allow himself to think in that way. He took in the beautiful view savoring every precious second before endeavoring on this precarious journey.

With no time to lose, he climbed into the boat, strapped on his three safety restraints, put on his helmet, and lowered his triple thick goggles. He went over his mental checklist, and then started the engine; it roared to a start, and then purred like a kitten as it idled. Next, he checked all the gauges, making sure everything was in proper working order. He flipped the switch to his transceiver and made a call to Abigail.

"Hey, Hon, this is your hubby Timmy, do you read me? Over."

"Yes, I read you, big lug! Please be careful, over."

"I will; I love you, over," he answered. He was ready to begin; he flipped the switch that engaged the big propeller. It made a whooshing sound as it started to spin, displacing a great deal of water. Mechanico Man pulled back lightly on the throttle and moved away from the dock towards the middle of the lake.

By putting Masterpiece One in the middle, he would have one hundred or so yards on either side from the shore. He would increase his speed so that by the time he reached the concrete plant he would be going the maximum. The concrete plant was about three miles south from his starting point. In total the lake was about eight miles in length, so he felt he had plenty of time to accelerate, then slow down enough to turn around and cruise back at a normal safe speed; at least for him, it would be normal.

As he started, everything went as planned. The engine and boat performed flawlessly. Feeling confident, he pushed the throttle to full. Except for a few local runs and tests at the shop, Mechanico Man had never tried pushing the boat to this point. He began to build speed, speed like he had never experienced; the rush had him reeling with delight. He was virtually pinned to his seat like someone in a G-force machine. At the speed he was traveling along with RPM's from the giant engine roaring, people near the lake were awakened. In their pajamas or whatever they slept in, they started running outside to see where the noise and commotion was coming from.

Mechanico Man never told anyone but his wife of the exact test date, not even his best friend Zippo Freeman. Later most would say they'd never heard anything like that sound in all their years living by the lake. The propeller was creating gigantic waves; the boat was traveling at a speed according to legend that was close to the speed of sound.

One of the things that Mechanico Man hadn't planned on was the size of those waves the giant propeller was creating. They completely obstructed his side vision, something he hadn't planned for; eyewitnesses say they were over thirty five feet high, although that's hard to substantiate because they were not very close to the lake. At that time the lake shores were not populated, extremely fortunate, as damage was minimal.

The fact he couldn't see meant that he had to guess where the concrete plant was located so he could slow down. With all the technology he had, he'd failed to install a gauge that would help him navigate if he couldn't see! He never imagined this would happen; besides, by this time, all the gauges on his boat were pegged to wide open. He had no idea how fast he was going or where he was situated in the lake!

He tried communicating with Abigail, but it was useless. She couldn't hear him, anyway. Again according to legend, he was at least six miles down the lake. By now, Mechanico Man knew he was in big trouble; he tried to slow the boat, but the throttle jammed and the boat just kept gaining speed as it headed toward the south shore. Also upon passing the concrete plant, the waves had become so high that the water they created caused a small tsunami and washed the piles of concrete material into the lake.

With a sucking action, the material was dragged behind Masterpiece One past the concrete plant and down the lake. Combined with the fact that he was traveling at a very high rate of speed, the huge propeller now spinning out of control, and the high waves, what happens from this point on is extremely vague. As legend goes, by the time he reached the end of the lake, he was still going at a tremendously high speed; he never slowed down!

One lone eyewitness, a twelve-year-old boy who was climbing a tree in the woods about one quarter mile away, said Mechanico Man's boat looked like a rocket ship on the water. The boat rammed into the shore, plowing into the land, extending the lake approximately another three miles. With his boat, the waves alongside him filled in the newly-plowed lakebed with fresh water. With the concrete already in the lake, a beautiful natural dam was formed. The electric company would eventually use it for their dam in the newly-enlarged lake to supply electricity.

Tim "Speed" Boatman, alias Mechanico Man, and his boat Masterpiece One were never seen again. His wife Abigail, although greatly saddened, was positive he would return. To this day, she keeps her transceiver on, hoping she'll hear his voice once again.

In honor of his amazing endeavor and creation,

the name 'Tim's Ford Lake and Dam' was given. They say if you look up into the trees at the end of the newly formed lake, you can see tiny particles of glittering metal hanging from their branches.

Abigail Boatman still hasn't given up hope; listening to the transceiver, hoping from the steady hum some kind of sound will come through the channel tuned to her husband's frequency.

"Let's look at the facts," she says to herself half-aloud. "There was nothing at the scene except a small fragment of titanium on the ground and all those particles in the trees."

She touches a small box containing the titanium, as she's done countless times before. Still a close friend of Abigail, Zippo Freeman, has his own theory. Zip, as everyone calls him, is a futurist and science fiction aficionado. Through much study and calculation, Zip feels that Mechanico Man was thrust into another dimension due to the high rate of speed he was traveling at the time of impact.

He theorizes that upon impact, instead of slowing down, Mechanico Man and his boat actually sped up, thereby causing a dimensional shift. At that point the boat disintegrated, leaving only what was left in the trees and the piece Abigail has in her possession. This would make perfect sense since according to his theory, only humanoid materials could make the shift. Zip wasn't totally sure of that, as he told Abigail it was possible that Tim and boat shifted or only Tim's subtle body made it through to the other dimension.

Chapter #2

Tim found himself exactly where he last remembered, at the very edge of the lake where he went hurling into space; it was also about the same time in the morning, although he had no idea of the day or date. He was in his Mechanico Man uniform, which felt much different, almost as if it was part of his own body, strange but not uncomfortable. The uniform was much different than the one he designed.

The 'new' Mechanico Man

"A real technological upgrade," he thought. The uniform was amazing; it contained a built-in computer, cell phone, and a multifunction device called a Zune. The material, no matter how hard Tim tried, could not be torn, scratched, or discolored. On both sides of the uniform there were practically invisible "zippered" breast pockets; over the right pocket, sewn in a space-age thread, were the words "Mechanico Man."

When Tim tried opening the pockets, it was if they almost opened on their own. Inside the left pocket was a piece if paper with instructions. Tim unfolded the note and read the instructions anxiously.

"Tim 'Speed' Boatman, alias Mechanico Man, when you read this, we hope you are feeling well with an open mind as to what you are about to experience. You are the same person you were before your 'experiment,' but then again, you're not. When you are ready, please refer to the computer mechanism on your person for further instructions. It will function as any other computer you are accustomed to: thank you and good luck."

At the time Mechanico Man had his experience, computers were huge bumbling pieces of machinery he'd read about in his magazines and catalogs; why, the cassette player in Masterpiece One was just brought onto the market when he installed the device. He remembered he was so excited about a tape player that wasn't bulky and played music for up to two hours, he just had to have one. Feeling something in his upper right hand pocket he reached in to retrieve the object; taped on it were two words, "cell phone."

He opened the phone and while it looked strange to him, he was knowledgeable enough to figure out how to use it.

"I hope Zip's phone number is the same," he thought. He pushed the numbers and then hit the button that read "send"; a slight pause, and the phone began ringing on the other end. After what seemed like endless rings, a voice answered.

"Hello." It was Zip!

"Hello," Zip repeated, "is anyone there?"

Mechanico Man finally summoned the energy to speak: "Zip, it's me, Tim." His own voice sounded strange.

"Is this some kind of prank?" Zip protested. "Tim Boatman has been gone for years! Besides, I don't recognize the voice."

"Years—I've been gone for years? Look, Zip, it is me; the fact that my voice sounds strange is just the icing on the cake. I've just read a note in my pocket that says it's me but not me, for starters. In fact, I don't know where to begin except I think it might have something to do with your dimensional stuff! Can you come up to the lake and meet me where I was last seen?"

Zip knew Tim was one of the few people that listened to him and his dimensional theories; in fact, Zip only mentioned this "stuff" to people he could trust. Still, he had to be cautious.

"If you are who you say you are, what is your wife's name, her birthday, and when were you married?"

"That's easy, Zip; my beautiful wife's name is Abigail, her birthday is November twentieth, and we were married on June seventh, 1981, in the herb garden behind our home. You were the best man, Zip!"

46

Zip just about could not contain himself. "It is you! Does Abigail know—have you told her you're back?"

"No, Zip, I kind of just showed up here and I don't want anyone to know or see me until I figure out some things. I need your help, Zip."

"I'll be right there, ole buddy, even though you never told me about your now infamous boat ride."

"Sorry Zip, I guess I should have told my closest and best friend."

"Stay put! We'll have plenty of time to catch up."

Zip showered, dressed, and headed to the lake. His wife Crystal was still sleeping soundly when he kissed her tenderly on the forehead and quietly slipped out the back door. It took Zip about fifteen minutes to reach the rendezvous point Tim mentioned. When he got there, he got out of his truck and began to call for Tim.

"Tim, Tim where are you? Hey Mechanico Man, show yourself, you bum!" Mechanico Man summoned the courage and stepped out from behind a huge oak tree.

"It's me, Zip." Zippo Freeman must have looked as if he had seen a ghost or strange apparition; never in his life did expect to see what was before his eyes.

Standing before him was a huge figure about eight feet tall; the fabric on his uniform was astounding. It quivered when you looked at it, and above the right breast pocket were the words "Mechanico Man"; they almost seemed electric. Then there were all the electronic devices distributed throughout the uniform but within arm's reach for the wearer.

"T-Tim, is that you? Take off your mask so I can see you."

"Therein lies the problem, my friend. I can't." Tim continued, "In my left pocket was a brief note describing my situation; it says to refer to the computer mechanism on my uniform. Wait a minute, Zip, I do know how to use it! I just didn't know how to access the information, seems I just have to concentrate on the task and the solution will come to me. I guess that's how the strange phone was no problem for me to use. Anyway, I'm glad you're here; we can experience this together."

Zip stepped closer, admiring the magnificent uniform with all of the devices; he touched the sleeve. It was like something he'd never felt before.

"Pretty neat huh? I still don't believe it myself. Well, let's find out what I'm all about." Mechanico Man pushed the on switch and the small computer came to life.

A screen appeared from out of the uniform; the material seemed to part and there appeared an LCD screen. The screen flashed and blinked as gigabytes of information were downloaded into the computer; it was if the information were coming from outer space. Zip watched in awe.

"I've never seen anything like this."

"That makes two of us; and the crazy thing is it's part of me!"

After a few minutes, a figure appeared on the screen; he was dressed in a jumpsuit type of uniform, basically the same material as Mechanico Man's, except his was trimmed with electric blue edging around the collar, sleeves, and leg bottoms. The shoes or boots were molded into the uniform. He looked humanoid but had a lion-like mane for hair; he seemed very tall.

Sarsun, Head of the Council of Planets

He possessed a warm smile and began to speak. "Tim Boatman, alias Mechanico Man, and Zippo Freeman, yes, I know you are both present and that is acceptable. I hope you are well and at peace. I am called Sarsun. Mechanico Man, Zippo will be your 'point' man and partner from now on."

Tim and Zip just looked at each other.

"We have made ourselves present through your primitive technology, although we have made some modifications to your devices to make them more useful. You are both about to embark on a journey that will save your planet; it will be one of many. Mechanico Man, when you came to us through a dimensional shift, you were basically destroyed; we reassembled you so you could reenter your own existence. When scanning your brain waves we found you to be intelligent, possessing exceptional character and capable of many technological skills. We also felt you were fearless, brave, and sometimes foolish, but brave men must sometimes possess this quality. Zippo, you were chosen because of your knowledge of other dimensions and computer savvy."

Almost in unison they asked, "Can we tell our wives?"

"Yes, that is permissible, but should the secret ever be exposed, then Mechanico Man would cease to exist. You have much more to learn about your new powers, Mechanico Man; however, daylight is coming to your planet. You should not be seen this way, at least not yet. Open your cell phone; do you see the button with no marking present? Press it twice and you will become Tim Boatman. When you want to transform to Mechanico Man press the same button twice again; you must have the cell phone with you at all times."

"That won't be unusual; everyone does that nowadays," Zip inserted.

"Zippo, when you go back to your home, you will find a special laptop computer, which is the lifeline between you and Mechanico Man. I will contact you by the special cell phone for further instructions. Mechanico Man, stay happy, enjoy life, and above all, peace; Sarsun out."

The computer screen disappeared; both men stood there almost as if they couldn't believe what transpired. Mechanico Man was still in his uniform. Almost without thinking, Mechanico Man pushed the special button twice on his cell phone; faster then the eye could see, he was again Tim Boatman, an older and wiser-looking Tim Boatman, sharply dressed, we might add. The two men hugged as old friends reunited.

"Let's go home."

"I'm with you," said Zip. They hopped into Zip's pick up truck and headed home.

Chapter #3

They arrived at Tim's house after a short ride from the south end of Tim's Ford Lake. During the ride, Tim told Zip he couldn't believe they named the lake and dam after him. Zip asked how they could not name it after him after that amazing speedboat ride he took so many years ago. Tim told Zip at this point the boat ride was rather vague to him. They pulled into Tim's driveway; everything looked about the same. Aside from a new front door, the house being painted a different color, the shrubs and trees having grown to maturity, it looked like home.

"I'd better go in and give the news to Abigail first, no telling how she'll take this, Tim. I'll signal for you to come in." Tim nodded in agreement, although he couldn't contain the excitement to see his beloved Abby again.

Zip went to the back door off the patio; it was out of the way so she wouldn't notice Tim, which might have taken place if she accidentally looked out the front door had he tried to enter there. When he got to the patio, he didn't have to knock, as Abigail was in the back yard working in one of her prized herb gardens. This surprised Zip; it was before seven o'clock in the morning. She noticed Zip approach.

"Good morning Zip, what brings you here so early?"

"Just in the area, Abby, thought I'd stop by for some of that good organic coffee you brew. "

"Great, I have some brewing right now; let's go inside."

Abigail washed her hands and set out two cups, then poured the fresh coffee; she proceeded to get half and half out of the fridge.

"So what's up, Zip?" she asked, a bit apprehensive.

"Abby, how ya' feeling these days?"

"Now Zippo Freeman, you know aside from me missing that crazy husband of mine, I'm doing just fine!"

Zip kind of shifted uneasily in his kitchen chair not knowing how to begin. "I received an unusual phone call this morning, one I'd couldn't imagine receiving, Abby; it was from somebody we both know."

"OK, Zip, don't go playing games with me; must I call Crystal to find out what's going on here?"

"No, no, she doesn't know anything yet; she was asleep when I left."

"When you left, where did you go, Zip?"

"I was at the south end of the lake, Abby." Abigail's face turned white as a sheet; the expression on her face was almost blank.

"Why would you do that?"

"You'd better sit down." She was standing by the kitchen sink; she fumbled for a kitchen chair and sat at the table. Zip figured he might as well keep the explanation as simple as possible, figuring Tim would eventually explain everything himself.

"I saw Tim, Abby." He reached out and grabbed her hand.

Before he could say anything else, she asked, "Is this one of your dimensional visions, Zip? You haven't been on one of your quests, have you?"

"No, Abby, it's really Tim." Zip had just about gotten the words out of his mouth when Abigail was up from the table and running out the front door towards Zip's truck; so much for the signal. By this time, Tim had gotten out of the truck as he couldn't sit any longer; he noticed Abigail rushing towards the door. Before you could say "Mechanico Man," they were both running toward each other, tears streaming down their faces; without a word, they embraced. Zip quietly got into his truck, slipped out of the driveway and headed home; neither Tim or Abigail noticed.

Finally after several minutes, Abigail spoke.

"How is this possible—how are you here? You look wonderful!"

"You look more ravishing and beautiful than the last time I saw you, Abby. It's an unusual story, one I'm still learning myself; I'll tell you all I know. Come on, let's go inside." They held each other arm in arm and headed toward the house.

Tim thought, "I don't know how long I've been gone, seems just like yesterday, but it's great to be home."

Tim had been back about a month; now he spent most of his time between the house and dock enjoying the lake and the love of his life, Abigail. He told Abigail everything he knew, including the fact that no one must know his secret. It wouldn't be difficult anyway, as the area had changed quite a bit since he was last there. Most of the folks he associated with had moved away or passed on. His boat repair shop had been turned into a boat rental.

Tim hadn't made contact with Sarsun since that first day he came back to the lake. He talked with Zip several times; Zip said the new laptop Sarsun gave him was awesome, although he had received nothing unusual. They both decided they shouldn't take on any new ventures as they both sensed the time was getting near when they would be called to action.

Abigail had mixed feelings about Tim's new plight, but she was so glad to have him back, she felt she could deal with anything. In the meantime, they were spending all their time together enjoying each other's company. On several evenings the two couples had lakeside dinners, talking into the night about old times and when something was going to take place. They wouldn't have to wait much longer. As the sun was setting several evenings after their last gathering, Tim felt his cell phone vibrate; it was Sarsun. Tim anxiously put the phone to his ear.

Chapter #4

"Greetings, Tim, I hope you are well and at peace. Have you adjusted fully to being back into your existence?"

"Hello Sarsun, greetings to you; yes, everything is wonderful. I was beginning to wonder when I would hear from you."

"We wanted to give you time to get reacquainted with Abigail and life in general. We now feel it is time for you to get into action as we need your services." This was the first time Tim actually noticed Sarsun say we; plus, it seemed as if he could read his thoughts.

"Do you feel you are ready, Tim?"

"Yeah, sure, Sarsun, ready as I'll ever be; one thing, Sarsun, when I become Mechanico Man I'm not sure how to function or what to do. Will I sense everything as I did before when I had the uniform on?"

"Yes remember the note said you would be the same and not the same; this is part of that scenario. Don't worry; everything will come to you as needed, plus the devices on your uniform will give all the information you require for each assignment. Eventually you will find you won't need the devices; your internal programming will take over and the devices will no longer be in your uniform. Plus, don't forget your friend Zippo will be there for you. I will say this; there will be occasions where you will be pushed to the limit, but then you seem to enjoy that. Besides, who wants to mess with an eight foot humanoid?"

This was the first humor Tim heard from Sarsun; he laughed quietly.

"Transform yourself to Mechanico Man within the next fifteen minutes and I will contact you then; Sarsun out."

The phone went silent; Tim walked toward the house to inform Abigail. They held each other and kissed lightly; Abigail's eyes were filled as she tried to hold back the tears. She didn't want to lose her man again.

"Don't worry, Abby, I'll be back. You have to look at this as my job; it's a job where I travel. I have the feeling it could be anywhere in the universe. Besides, you can always find out what's going on by contacting Zip; he'll be in constant communication with me." He leaned and kissed her again.

"I know," she said, "I know," and she touched his hand. Tim looked at her sweetly walked outside and pushed the blank button on his cell phone twice; in an instant, he was gone.

Zip was sitting at his desk when his computer screen lit up like a Christmas tree. It was downloading information so fast it looked like a continuous blur.

Zippo Freeman at his new laptop

"I'll bet Bill Gates would like to know these guys!" he said aloud. "It's happening," Zip sensed, "Tim is now Mechanico Man." He sat glued to the screen waiting for further instructions; his intuition told him Mechanico Man was no longer on Earth. The computer screen finally stopped whirling and Sarsun appeared.

"Greetings, Zip, I hope you are well and at peace."

57

"Greetings, Sarsun; thank you, the same back to you. What's going on?"

"In a moment, you and Mechanico Man will receive these signals simultaneously as will be the case on every assignment. Now I must acclimate Mechanico Man to his surroundings; however, you will also receive the transmission."

Meanwhile, Mechanico Man had already figured out his devices; instead of having to receive information from the computer and the bulky screen, he routed it through the Zune with its smaller screen, plus the headphone speakers were already in his helmet.

"Good, Mechanico Man, I see you're already figuring out your devices; I told you this would happen."

"Great! Sarsun, where in the universe am I?" Mechanico Man seemed preoccupied.

"In a moment, Mechanico Man; Zippo, are you receiving this?"

"Yes, Sarsun, loud and clear; hey, Mechanico Man, I can see and hear you. I'd like to know where you are—sure ain't Tennessee."

"I know the two of you know hardly anything of me or where I originate from, that will come in due time, my friends. This much I will tell you; all who live here on my planet are beings of peace. The name of the planet is Auroari; it is located near the edge of our universe. As I'm sure you know, a planet of peace does not just happen; it comes after millennia of struggle and strife. The reason for me telling you this is that I want the both of you to know many of the situations you are involved in will at the moment seem to go against anything that resembles peace; hopefully in time, the end result will however be peace."

"This brings us to your first assignment; I'm sure both of you are familiar with the Roswell, New Mexico incident of 1947. The crash of an alien vessel and the recovery or capture of alien beings— even today on your planet this event is being discussed, although your government likes to keep things like this a great secret. Mechanico Man, you are in the outer area of the planet's atmosphere where these beings, sometimes referred to as the 'Grays,' exist. Don't worry you are not detectable by any of their tracking equipment or devices. Don't you just love your new suit, Mechanico Man?"

Zip broke in: "I'm sure our government would like to get a hold of that suit, Sarsun."

"I'm sure they would. Let me continue; the name of this planet is Rahufoya the u is long sounding as in the word *you*. You and your countrymen have not been told the truth about the Roswell incident. I hope neither of you will be offended, but you are still a very primitive people. Your world leaders are so proud, yet they are constantly at war, but that is another story."

"When the Grays visited your planet in 1947, they did not only visit the United States; many ships did reconnaissance all over the planet. They were on a mission of observation and peace. When their ship crashed at Roswell, two of their astronauts were alive when they were brought into captivity by your armed forces. They were not treated well and were dissected and tortured in the name of science."

"Why didn't they let us know of their mission?" Mechanico Man asked. For the first time since their meeting, Sarsun seemed to laugh.

"Mechanico Man, have you never watched Star Trek, the prime directive? No interference with lesser developed cultures, come on now! Anyway, back to why you are here. You have heard of all the abductions by the Grays; this was in retaliation for the incident at Roswell. Naturally, two wrongs do not make a right. In fact, several years ago, the Council of Planets banned the beings of Rahufoya from further encounters with the people of Earth."

"There's a Council of Planets? Well, I'll be," blurted Mechanico Man.

"I've heard of that in my studies" added Zip.

"Yes, actually most of your work will be through the Council. Anyway, the Grays did not heed the Council's warnings and that is why you are here. Your mission, should you decide to accept it, Mechanico Man, oh, I'm sorry; I've been watching too many of your Mission Impossible reruns from the satellites. Actually, Mechanico Man, we need you to go in and disable their communication system and fuel production plant. They only have one fuel production facility as this is a small planet. This will keep them from space flight hopefully for several months, enabling the Council to use other means of getting through to them."

"Is there any danger?" Mechanico Man asked.

"Of course there is danger!" Sarsun responded. "Once the assignment begins the Council will not acknowledge any association with the two of you"

"This *is* like Mission Impossible," Zip thought.

"Instructions, coordinates, anything else you could possibly need will be there for you. Between the two of you, I'm not going to say it will be easy, but it is do-able. As for the danger part, Mechanico Man, you are going to be amazed at the ability of the uniform and its protection. By the way, never lift your mask, especially on this planet; the atmosphere is mostly hydrogen oxide. Sarsun out."

"I can lift my mask?" Mechanico Man thought.

Chapter #5

Without touching the keyboard, Zip's laptop was downloading information for this assignment; Mechanico Man was receiving information at the same time. It seemed much of the information was being downloaded right into his brain, an unusual sensation to say the least. He mentioned this to Zip.

"You know they say we only use ten to fifteen percent of our brain capacity; I guess the other eighty five to ninety percent of yours is being put to use" Zip answered. "I'm getting satellite images of the fuel plant and communication array; you getting anything, Mechanico Man?"

"Yes, I can see the images, but in my head!"

"Cool," Zip responded. About this time, two things occurred to Mechanico Man. One, he was floating in outer space and had to figure out how to navigate.

Two: "Zip, instead of addressing me as Mechanico Man all the time, how about shortening it to Mech, like tech? The long way sounds so formal, and after all, we are best friends. Hey, I'm getting flight instructions on my Zune!"

"Great, Mech, let's work on our plan of action— seems night is coming to the two locations."

"Let's see if we can call up a map and diagram of the locations; my feeling is we're going to disable both locations at the same time, since it will lessen my chance of getting snagged. Wow, this suit has an invisible mode. I feel better already!"

"Mech, let's get through this before we talk about our feelings. I have to tell you that even though you say you're invisible, I can still see you on my computer screen. You look sort of the way I tell you I see subtle entities; you're there, but kind of transparent. Probably a safety mechanism so I'll know your position at all times. Anyway, I think it's time you head down to the planet and check out the situation."

"Agreed. As long as they don't see me, I'm glad you can, Zip." With that being said, Mechanico Man floated down through the atmosphere soundless and invisible, and landed silently on the surface about five hundred yards from the communication array.

What an unusual planet even at night! The ground was kind of a bluish gray, plant growth (if that's what you'd call it) was stunted and almost colorless, and two small odd-shaped asteroids floated in the sky reflecting a dull moonlight. The communication array surrounded a small building the diagram and map showed as the main power source for the array. There were two guards at the main entrance; if this invisible thing was going to work this would be the test.

"How ya going to get in once you get there?" Zip whispered in his headphones.

"I don't know; I'm sure it will come to me. Maybe being invisible means I can walk through walls and doors, too!" He approached the building, realizing the doorways were smaller than normal, only about five feet high and about two feet wide.

"This is not going to be easy for an eight foot person!" he relayed to Zip. He reached for the door knob and lo and behold—his hand went right through the door! He could walk right through! The guards didn't even notice, although being that close to his first aliens, especially the Grays, sent a chill down his spine. With their large heads, unblinking eyes, and small bodies, they looked menacing. Their overall color was about the same as his uniform.

"Must be universal," he thought. When he got inside, there wasn't much to see except a pinkish glow coming from a central room that was behind what seemed to be two lead-lined doors.

"What do you have for me, Zip?"

"I believe that's some kind of reactor; apparently it's potentially dangerous, as the room and doors are about ten inches thick and lined with some kind of special lead-type material. The reactor powers the entire planet's communication array including their satellites. Whatever they use is very volatile—you'll have to be extremely careful."

A message appeared on his Zune; it read, "Your suit can withstand Rahufoyan radiation for no longer than ten minutes."

"So this suit has limitations," he thought. Mechanico Man went through the doors; there was a control panel with instruction in a language he'd never seen. Actually, they were more like symbols than letters. Meanwhile, on Zip's computer, the instructions were being translated to English.

"Hold on, Mech, I'll have it for you in a second. OK, got it; oh boy, it's not going to be easy. With you having only ten minutes, it'll be close. The only way to disable the array totally is to get underneath the reactor; there you'll find five connections. You can't just disconnect them; they seemed to be melded into the reactor. It looks like they'll have to be blown apart with some kind of explosive."

Suddenly from directly inside Mechanico Man's head, he heard, "In your lower left leg pocket, you will find an explosive device capable of handling this task. There will be a detonation timer that can be set to detonate on command from Zip's computer."

"Did you get that message, Zip?"

"Sure, looks like I get to have some fun without leaving home."

"Don't rub it in, Zip. If it weren't for me you'd still be working in that stuffy office inputting data at the concrete plant. I'm going to try to get under the reactor; with these guys being so small, it's hard to maneuver."

Mechanico Man tried to position himself in every type of angle.

"A little help here, Zip!"

"I don't know what to tell you, except you're down to a minute on the suit protection!'

"Great! I wish the thing could make my arm extend." And with that, Mechanico Man's left arm extended, allowing him to place the explosives in perfect position.

"Get out of there Mech, twenty seconds!" Without thinking, Mechanico man scrambled to his feet and ran through the lined double doors.

"Whew, that was close."

"I'll say—I should have been sweating bullets, but I'm perfectly dry. Zip, the uniform is air-conditioned!"

"That's good, 'cause I did enough sweating for both of us! No time to lose, Mech, let's get going with part two, the fuel production plant."

Chapter #6

The fuel plant was about eighty miles southwest from the communication array; Mechanico Man made it to the location in about eight seconds again, landing very softly and silently.

"Seems like I'm rocket-propelled without all the fire and sound..."

Suddenly a message transmitted on his Zune:

"You are propelled by a technology unknown to your planet; it is called 'energy propulsion.'"

Zip received the same message. "I'll tell you, Mech, this uniform stuff is never-ending; it's mind boggling! This place is really guarded; surveillance and many more guards, and they have towers around the whole perimeter."

"Yeah, and it's about three times the size of the other place. I'll bet this won't be as easy to disable."

"We still have about four hours of darkness. Speaking about two wrongs not making a right, I don't know about you, Mech, but we're going to have to distract these guards and get them out of harm's way. Looking at the complex, it seems the entrance gate is the furthest point from the plant; maybe we can cause a distraction to draw them to the gate. You're still invisible."

"So we have two situations here: the guards, and the plant itself. You see those strange-looking vehicles over there; you think we can commandeer one to the gate?"

Within seconds, Mechanico Man was trying to read the insignia on the front of the vehicle: "Hey Zip it's called a, wait a minute—I can't' unscramble that gibberish; it's those symbols again!"

Again, within seconds, through Mechanico Man's eyes and Zip's computer, the "gibberish" was translated. The information on the vehicle was downloaded onto Zip's computer.

"I'll see if we can access the vehicle codes and move it towards the front gate." It was as if Zip and Mech were thinking as one.

"By the way, in English the vehicle is called a Ford!"

"Real funny, can we move this thing?"

"It's some kind of hover vehicle; aren't you getting the info also?"

"Yeah, Zip, I sure am; they're coming right into my head! Just to be safe, you relay the instructions to me; I'm at the vehicle."

"Here goes; you see the symbols on the left side panel? Tap them just as I tell you. The second symbol, tap it twice; the fourth symbol, once; the sixth symbol; three times, and the last one once."

Mechanico Man tapped the symbols as Zip called them out; suddenly a door appeared and slid open.

"How can entities that look so menacing be so advanced?" Mechanico Man thought to himself. Once the door opened, a console array lit up before him on what appeared to be a dashboard; however, there was no steering device.

"Now what? Can we move this thing by remote control?"

"Hang on, Mech, I'm getting the answers now. OK, yes, we can move it remotely; I'll have to do that from here, but first you must activate the vehicle's propulsion system."

"OK, shoot, which is what I hope they don't start doing when this thing fires up."

"Remember, Mech, you're invisible."

"Right, but as yet we don't know if I'm bullet or laser proof, whatever comes out of those weapons they're holding."

"You see that diamond-shaped symbol at the

bottom left of the console? Push and hold it down."
The hover vehicle seemed to come to life without a
sound.

"Wow, so far, so good, Zip; now what?"

"About the middle of the console there should be
a symbol resembling an arrow; actually there's two
of them, side by side. One is for forward, the other
backward. Push the one furthest to the right."

"Hey, not that much different than our way of
doing things!"

"Brilliant, Mech—now pay close attention or
you're liable to be hauled away with the vehicle. In
order for me to move the vehicle remotely, you must
enter a code into the array. According to my
information, each vehicle has its own unique code;
don't mess up, man!" As Zip called out the symbols
to him, Mechanico Man seemed to follow, almost as
if he was programmed to do so. Good thing, as the
code was long and complicated; after what seemed
like a couple of minutes, the code was fed into the
console array.

"You did great Mech; this last set of symbols will
close the side of the vehicle."

"Well, now that that's over with, let's get back to
the serious work. Hopefully none of these guards
will notice that thing running." With that,
Mechanico Man listened to his Zune for
instructions as to where to enter the complex. The
message he heard was to follow the instructions Zip
would relay to him, for like the hover vehicle, it
would be easier for him to listen, and then perform
the needed tasks.

"I'm in your hands, Zip," Mechanico Man waited for a response.

"You see those doors right under the two tallest guard towers? That's where you have to enter; it's your quickest access. Mech I'm sensing some kind of heat detection as part of their protection system; their body temperature is about twenty degrees lower than ours, and that extra heat might set something off. Is there anything you can do to offset the difference?"

Mechanico Man accessed a temperature control on his suit and proceeded to lower the temperature thirty degrees; for once he was slightly uncomfortable.

"I hope I can handle this, Zip; it's chilly!"

"Better you're chilly than detected by those guys; seems like from what we know, they don't like to mess around."

Lowering his suit temperature worked and Mechanico Man was able to get inside the complex. Once inside, he realized this would not be easy. Although totally automated, there were laser beams pointing in every direction, weight triggered alarms on the floor, and many panels displaying the same type of symbols as in the hover vehicle. What was even more challenging is that there seemed to be objects that looked liked microphones everywhere. This meant even the slightest sound would set off the alarms.

Zip was the first to speak. "Hey Mech those things that look like microphones, real sensitive too! I'd advise you to not speak unless you absolutely have to and then at the quietest whisper."

"I hope those microphones can't detect my teeth chattering," Mechanico Man thought.

"I heard that!" Zip almost yelled. It made Mechanico Man shrug his shoulders like his ears hurt.

"Thanks partner that's all I need is to be hard of hearing and cold!" Again Mechanico Man did not speak.

"This is great Mech, somebody is definitely looking out for us. I better not speak, either." Zip thought the last statement.

"I heard you too!' Mechanico Man thought back. So now they were still able to communicate by a kind of telepathy, but why was Mechanico Man so cold? If everything else seemed to work, then why not the adjustment for the cooler temperature?

Chapter #7

Zip communicated new instructions to Mechanico Man: "Mech, in order for you to get past the lasers, I'm going to disable them from here." Zip input codes that were put on the screen into his laptop and voila, it was done.

"The guards that are monitoring them will think they are still working. I've actually superimposed a video of them working onto their screen. You're going to have to use your propulsion system to get over the floor alarms."

"I figured that, thing is where am I going?" It

seemed strange to not have to use your voice to communicate, but the both of them adjusted.

"You have to get yourself to the other side of the panels; it seems you're going to have to do your work from the maintenance access area. If you can maneuver to the far end of this first room, there will be another door that will get you into the maintenance area."

"Here goes." With no controls on his uniform, Mechanico Man knew he was going to have to maneuver himself mentally as before. He knew he had to concentrate; there was no room for error.

He thought, "Slowly, carefully, stay calm and don't panic." He began to move across the room towards the far end and actually forgot about being cold. As he moved carefully across the room, he noticed there was no let up in security; the fuel production facility must be of great priority on this planet. Maybe this protection was against some of their own citizens. He reached the far end of the room there was about two feet of space where he could land in front of the door; normally the lasers would have protected this area. How was he to know what was on the other side? Suddenly he realized another feature of being Mechanico Man; he could see through walls!

"Seems like every time I'm confronted with another problem, Zip, I discover some other feature. There is another two-foot section on the other side of the door; I'm goin' through."

"You know, sometimes I wonder why I'm even involved, Mech; you seem to have everything under control."

"Not so, Zip, I need you; you confirm what I'm thinking. I'm going to go with the two heads are better than one theory; I couldn't do it without you, friend. Besides, how quickly you forget you're my lead man, especially in this situation, and remember Sarsun said we were partners."

"Thanks, ol' buddy, you know how I get insecure at times. We'd better speed it up; we only have two hours of darkness." As they were having this conversation information appeared on Zip's screen.

"OK, Mech, here's the situation; you have get yourself to the center console which is about one hundred yards from where you're located."

"It's really tight in here, Zip; there's probably no more than two feet from the panels to the opposite wall. One hundred yards, that's a football field, and if I try to hover, I'll hit the suspended microphones."

"You'd better think about shrinking."

"See, Zip, that's why I need you!" Mechanico Man thought about being smaller and was compressed enough so he could hover through the area without hitting the microphones.

"Weird," he thought.

"I know," responded Zip.

"I'm here; now what do you have for me?"

"This console controls the whole production facility; it's kind of like the main circuit breaker in our electrical boxes at home. The problem is you can't just shut it down; if you shut down one part, another backup system comes on line. I guess that's why it has to be blown apart."

"Yeah, Zip, but from the looks of this place, I

mean even from here I see all kinds of pipelines and vat-type containers through observation ports. They must contain raw materials and finished fuel. If we blow this thing, I think were going to have a lot more than just a local explosion—looks like the whole place will go."

"I'm sure of it Mech, especially with what just came up on the computer screen." On the screen appeared an exit route Mechanico Man had to use; he was to get out of the facility while Zip triggered the explosive devices for both locations. Plus, before they detonated the explosions, they needed to distract the guards with the hover vehicle so no one would be hurt.

"Hey Zip, what about the two guards at the communication facility?"

"According to the information I'm receiving, it will be a shift change, so no one will be near the building; the shift is made at the main gate, which is far enough away so that all they'll have to do is seek shelter in the gatehouse."

"You mean that weird looking dome I saw while I was landing there? It must be made of something special; it didn't seem that far away."

"I guess so. Anyway, here's where you being a mechanic is going to come in handy; you're going to earn your name, Mechanico Man. I hate to say this, Mech, but there is a certain amount of risk here; you have to disconnect and cross live connections. It's kind of like our electricity except it is very powerful—looks like they draw the energy from the center of the planet."

"That would make sense; didn't Sarsun say this planet was some kind of hydrogen? That's part of the chemical basis for electricity."

"Here's what you have to do; find the large connecting cables on the console. They run down the side and along the bottom of the console to a large junction near the floor. You have to access those cables inside the junction."

"I see it, Zip; there seems to be another two-by-two area where I can stand. I'm going to hover into position; man, those are huge cables. There seems to be huge bolts or locks on this box plus some kind of electronic panel."

Mechanico Man at the electronic panel

"Yeah, Mech, the first thing we have to do is break the code. Wait; it's coming on the screen now. Do you see a small device that looks like bent key?"

"I see it, Zip."

"Turn it three times to the right, then once to the left, then back to center."

As Mechanico Man made the last turn, the panel came to life, showing the same symbols he'd seen on all the other devices the Grays used. Zip read the codes and Mechanico Man executed them perfectly; as he did what seemed to be a tool box rose out of the junction.

"That was the easy part; now you have to get ready to become the mechanic, but first I think I'd better create a distraction with the hover vehicle." Zip typed in the proper code and the hover vehicle headed toward the exit gate, its theft alarm screaming loudly. The vehicle did not take a straight path but careened wildly, causing the guards to be totally absorbed in finding out what had happened.

"Go, Mech!" Mechanico Man opened the tool box and saw a device that resembled a wrench that was configured to fit on the bolt-type locks. Mechanico Man was wondering how such frail beings could muster the strength to operate such a large tool on those huge locks.

"It's power operated, Mech."

At that point, Mechanico Man notice a switch-like device and flipped its position. He wasted no time loosening the locks with blurring speed. As they came apart, he placed them back inside the box the tool came from as space was at a premium. Only two would fit into the box; the other four he had to lay on the floor around him.

"Not much room to work, partner; I hope this doesn't get too complicated." Neither of them could keep their thoughts private, so Zip didn't allow what he wanted to think into his mind.

Instead he thought, "We only have a limited amount of time before the Grays catch on, Mech; here's what you have to do." Luckily the cables were color-coded, probably so that in case of emergency anyone in the facility could perform whatever was needed to keep the plant up and running. The colors were slightly different but close enough to identify with standard color names.

"Mech, disconnect the two bluish cables and place them in the blank slots to the left bottom of the junction. Because the whole operation is automated, it will take several minutes before anyone realizes something has changed. Now remove the reddish color cables and quickly place them where the blue ones were originally. Take the blue cables out of the blanks and place them where the red ones were." Suddenly the almost-silent operation of the plant became alive with a whirl, the type of sound you hear when something is overloaded. Something told Mechanico Man to reach into the same left leg pocket as he did at the communication array. There was another small explosive device.

"Place it on top of the cables and get out of there,

Mech; you'll have approximately three minutes! At that time I'm going to detonate both of the devices at each location; hurry! I'll program the exit route into your Zune." Zip tried not to sound excited even though they were still communicating through thought.

In the meantime, the whirl had become ear-splitting. The guards were down at the exit gate as the hover vehicle crashed into it and burst into flames. As they had thought, the guards figured with all the automated security the plant would be safe if they left it for a few minutes; suddenly the noise from the plant roused their attention. Mechanico Man could not waste any time, as the guards already realized something was wrong; he plowed right through everything. As he was still invisible, walls and communication arrays were not a problem.

Then something did go wrong; it had only been about a minute when a loud explosion erupted inside the fuel plant. Mechanico Man was engulfed in flames and was hurled at great speed towards a giant vat full of raw fuel; he looked down and he was totally visible! Zip instinctively detonated the explosive device at the communication array; then his computer screen went blank.

Chapter #8

Zip was shouting at the blank screen, "Mechanico Man, are you there? Talk to me, Mech, come on! Tim, where are you!"

In an instant the screen came to life. "Greetings, Zip; I hope you are well and at peace."

"Get real, Sarsun; where is my friend? The last thing I saw on my computer screen was a ball of flame and Mechanico Man hurtling through the air visible and engulfed in that flame!"

Almost as if to add a dramatic flare to what he would say next, Sarsun remained silent. Zip shifted nervously in his seat staring blankly at the screen with Sarsun's image.

Finally Sarsun spoke, "Your friend is fine and will return to you shortly. His ability to think while under extreme conditions saved him."

"You mean all the technology you gave him couldn't help?" Zip asked.

"Not in that particular situation; however, adjustments will be made for future altercations including the ten minute time limit on the suit for protection. I will leave you so he can tell you in his own words." With that, Zip's screen went blank again and almost simultaneously there was a knock on Zip's door.

Zip's feet hardly touched the floor! His wife Crystal couldn't even get out of her chair; she had come to sit by his side when she heard him yelling for his friend. Zip opened the front door.

"It's you!" The two men embraced; a sigh of relief came from the both of them as the assignment was over.

"What happened, Tim? How'd you get out of that mess?"

"It was easy; when I saw myself in that situation, I knew there was no way out, so I reached into my pocket, grabbed the cell phone and hit the blank button twice, and here I am. What else could I do? At least now I know why my uniform temperature stayed cool; that was a pretty warm situation! What I really want to know is were we successful?"

"Let's go to the computer and find out; I already spoke with Sarsun a few minutes ago." By the time they got to the computer the screen was coming alive; Sarsun was present.

"Greetings, my friends; I hope you are well and at peace." Sarsun was smiling, "Your assignment and mission was indeed a great success. The inhabitants of the planet Rahufoya have indeed been grounded. They have lost all communication on their planet and space travel has been brought to a standstill, all with no loss of life. Hopefully now we can persuade them to stop their nonsense. The two of you are to be commended; the Council of Planets is both pleased and grateful for your actions and accomplishments. Personally, in my many years as a mediator, counselor, and peacemaker, I have never seen two beings work so hard and well together; you are a great attribute to your species. I hope our future missions together will be as productive and fulfilling."

"I'd like to apologize for my behavior and attitude a while ago, Sarsun." Zip humbly replied.

"No need, my son; it is to be expected when someone cares so dearly about his friend. I would have expected nothing less."

"Sarsun, are there others like me who transform into something such as Mechanico Man?"

"Tim, you are unique in the universe; it is the

first time we've tried something of this nature. Then again, you are a unique personality. Until next time, I will leave you; stay happy, enjoy life, and above all peace. Sarsun out."

Tim and Zip sat quietly for a moment; Crystal was already on the phone telling Abigail that Tim had returned safely.

Finally Tim spoke. "It seems like I'm always asking you this, Zip, but could you take me home?"

"Sure, ol' buddy, I don't know how you'd get around without me." They laughed and got into Zip's pickup truck.

"Make it snappy, Zip, Abby's waiting."

To be continued...

O.C.I.
The Ocean City Italian

People who frequent Ocean City, New Jersey, know it's much more than a place for retired folks. It is a resort for fun and family no matter what age or ethnic background. It is a wonderful place to spend time with your family and friends. Here is a story that involves family, friendship and the wonderful experience of Ocean City.

It's funny how it all happened. Here we are in historic Ocean City, New Jersey, facing the beautiful Atlantic Ocean and sitting under a gazebo lined with newly painted wooden benches. Ten 'retired' Italians from Philadelphia, New York, and New Jersey are sitting and exchanging pastimes. Antonio Ventura spent many years counting numbers, but I don't think he was an accountant. Uncle Jimmy, as we all call him, was in an "intoxicating" business at a time when intoxicating wasn't allowed to be a business. There's Dominic the antique and art dealer, Phonograph Joe and the list goes on. You can imagine the colorful background of these gentlemen and their unique vocations, a breed that survived before laptop computers and cell phones. One morning watching the sunrise, when everyone was in a quiet, mellow mood I decided to recall a story that I thought all these gentlemen would enjoy.

After exchanging our morning greetings, I began: not so long ago, a beautiful woman had captured the heart of Franklin Armello, a man who had acquired his wealth much in the same way this group of men had acquired theirs. The woman was none other than Miss Madonna Temptation; she was a famous fashion model, seen on television, magazine ads, and billboards. She changed her name from Tempalatti for reasons one can only speculate, times being as they were.

The men's eyes brightened as they all knew of and had seen Miss Madonna Temptation.

Ms. Temptation in the meantime had no inkling of Franklin's feelings or for that matter of Franklin Armello. Anyway, Franklin had built an empire from various types of schemes and shady business corporations.

This brought smile to the faces of the men sitting under the gazebo as they continued to listen intently while sipping their morning coffee and enjoying fresh bagels.

All the while Franklin's love for Madonna held no bounds. He was going to do whatever it would take to meet her and capture her love. He started by sending her anonymous gifts and letters, extolling her beauty and fame. Finally, after several weeks with no response, he started signing his name, explaining who he was, and that he would do anything to meet and be with her.

Unfortunately again he was not successful in receiving a response from Ms. Temptation, only from her press agent, who mailed him a pre-signed eight-by-ten glossy of Ms. Temptation. Ms Madonna couldn't care less, as I said before; she didn't know of him. This really disturbed Armello, who was now totally and passionately absorbed in thought of his unattainable love. Neglecting his duties with his companies, he booked a flight to Beverly Hills California to find and visit with his love obsession.

Being the type of operator Franklin was, he had connections all over the country, including California, so he was able to obtain Ms. Temptation's address. Additionally he hired a private detective to keep track of her coming and going until he arrived.

This way he would know the precise time to call on her. Franklin also brought with him Lefty Gordono, his best "officer," in case he might run into any trouble or danger.

As I gazed at the men I could see them jokingly poking one another. "Trouble," one of them laughed.

206 Rodeo Drive was the address. The private detective told Franklin she would be home most days in the mid afternoon between 2:00 p.m. and 6:00 p.m.; the day Franklin arrived was no

exception. When he approached Ms Temptation's mansion, in front of him were two beautiful twelve-foot-high cast iron gates plus a gate house with two uniformed security guards.

Franklin approached the gates with Lefty at his side; a security guard came out of the gate house and asked if he could be of assistance to the two men. Franklin proceeded to tell the guard who he was and his reason for coming. The guard listened, then told Franklin he'd return momentarily.

Upon returning from the gate house, the guard had his partner with him. He told Franklin Ms. Temptation had no intention of allowing him to visit, for she did not know him personally, only vaguely from his many letters and gifts. Besides, the guard informed, she was in love with another man and they had planned to marry. She also told the guard to thank Franklin for all his kind gifts and letters, but please not to send anymore. This was standard procedure for adoring fans trying to get a glimpse of the beautiful Ms. Temptation.

Franklin was in shock; he was always used to getting his way, and in fact, he almost stormed the gate with Lefty but thought that would only be embarrassing as he was sure there were more guards within the mansion grounds. The last thing he wanted to do was upset his precious love. Dejected and heartbroken, he and Lefty returned home.

I could hear my friends grumbling; I even heard one of them say he would have stormed the gate.

Franklin never fully recovered from the situation

and, as happens with many corporations, even his, when the leader crumbles, so goes the corporation. Eventually Franklin lost everything, his companies, his status in the 'community', and his men. Lefty wound up trying to salvage what used to be a thriving business.

Due to his distraught, depressed, and careless attitude, he wasn't offered a position in any of his old businesses; really, he didn't give a hoot. At least Franklin had enough pride left that he would not let himself become homeless. He took a job delivering pizzas and found an apartment in the poorest section of town.

In the meantime, Madonna Temptation had gotten married and was now Mrs. Madonna Temptation-Silvers. She married the famous Hollywood director and producer Samuel Silvers; together they had a son, whom they named Samuel II. For the most part, her life was wonderful; she had a beautiful son and someone she loved dearly, not to mention that with the help of her new husband, she'd become the heart-throb queen of the big screen. She was a guest on many television programs including the Johnny Carson show. As for Franklin, he had all do to keep up his one room low-rent apartment.

My friends on the benches were still listening with undivided attention.

Franklin had begun a hobby that had become quite an obsession; seems he was an obsessive kind of guy. His job delivering pizzas gave him plenty of spare time and as he lived by the ocean most of his life, besides the beach and ocean breezes, he loved to fly kites. Almost any day, weather permitting, you can find someone flying a kite at the Jersey shore.

The men nodded in agreement as a few were seen dotting the early morning sky.

Franklin loved kites so much that he began building his own custom models. After work. he would spend most of his time designing and building these amazing kites; he'd become quite the master. Naturally, this took money for supplies, money he didn't have, so he would scrounge and scour the beach and boardwalk for the right size paper, wood, and other materials. Sometimes folks would donate materials for his kite making, as everyone, young and old, loved to watch his kites sail across the sky.

Over time, he had gained a reputation for his unusual and wonderful kites. In fact, Franklin became known as the "Kite Man." Every Saturday morning before work, he would take his flying masterpieces down to the beach and fly them over the ocean for hours. Even though Franklin was extremely poor and could have supplemented his income by selling his kites, he chose not to do so. His reasoning was that he didn't have to pay for the material to make them, so why charge someone to own one of his kites? Instead, when he was done flying them, he'd give them away to the children who had gathered to watch his display of magnificent kites. This was quite a change from a man who had garnered his wealth in unscrupulous ways in the past. Time, age, and a connection to his roots had mellowed Franklin Armello.

There was one kite Franklin would not give away; he called this kite "The Falcon." It was the only black kite in the sky. It brought delight to the young and old. He built it with wings that actually flapped; the tail was so well-designed that the kite would sail in the slightest breeze or heaviest gale. It had a golden beak that would open and close as if to swallow the clouds as it soared graciously across the sky. The wingspan was almost six feet, the length almost eight feet; this kite was a feat of engineering.

Franklin's prized Falcon Kite

It was almost 9:00 am by now my bench friends

should be going for their morning walk or boardwalk bike ride, but not today; they were still glued to my story.

In the meantime, the Madonna Temptation story: had taken a turn, a turn for the worse, I'm afraid. Madonna's husband, the now even more famous director and producer, decided it was time for a new starlet plaything to be made famous, and Madonna had to go. After months of tabloid scandals, there was a settlement and divorce between her and Mr. Silvers.

With her own prosperous career and the settlement, Madonna was a very wealthy woman. She also received full custody of Samuel II (Sammy), which was fine with her ex-husband, as he was more interested in his new "love."

Madonna was becoming tired of the glitter and glamour of Hollywood, so she decided to move to the east coast. I failed to mention this before, but Madonna Tempalatti, a.k.a. Madonna Temptation, was also a Jersey girl. So she and her son moved to (of all places) Ocean City, New Jersey. She felt she wanted to spend more quality time raising Sammy and that she could pick and choose her work, because with her great wealth there was no need to work all the time. Besides, New York was just a few hours away, and she could still model; she hadn't lost her girlish figure even after Sammy was born. She bought a beautiful but modest beach front house just past the southern end of the boardwalk.

The two situations of Franklin's and Madonna's lifestyle had crossed over so that they were actually in Ocean City at the same time.

If I didn't know better, I would have thought that my bench buddies were silently cheering; at least they didn't look as somber.

Madonna's son waited with great anticipation for Saturday to come so he could watch Franklin fly his kites. Sammy, being aware of his financial status, always remained in the back of the crowd, so when Franklin would give away his kites, other less fortunate boys and girls would get them. He used to come home and tell his mother about the Kite Man and his wonderful kites, especially the one called the "Falcon." Madonna would listen and promised one day to go with him to see the Kite Man and his wonderful kites.

The summer season passed quickly, autumn came, and Sammy entered a private school and was only home on weekends. He never missed watching Kite Man when weather permitted. Winter season came, Christmas had come and gone, and New Jersey was into one of the worst winters on record. Temperatures were almost always below freezing, shore dwellers thought they'd wake up one morning and see the ocean waves frozen in place. Needless to say, Franklin and his kites were not seen much during this time.

Now as fate would have it, Madonna's son came down with a rare illness from which he could possibly die. His mother took him to all the best doctors; they went to specialists in Philadelphia Pennsylvania, New York City, eventually both of them flew to San Diego, California, trying to find doctor or specialist who knew about this rare disease.

The conclusion from every doctor was that this disease couldn't be cured by traditional medicine. Exasperated, Madonna decided Sammy would have to go to an herbal specialist in Atlanta, Georgia. She had read a lot about Dr. Morton Yang and felt he might be able to get a grip on Sammy's affliction. In the meantime, Sammy was getting weaker by the day. Without wasting a moment, Madonna had them both on a flight to see this herbal healer.

Oh boy, my bench buddies are now pacing and leaning against the boardwalk railing; some are expressing their doubts with this herbal healer quack!

"C'mon, guys, give the doc a chance!"

I'd better keep this story rolling.

After a three hour session with Dr. Yang, Sammy seemed really drained,; combined with the flight to Atlanta, plus all the testing, he needed a rest. Dr. Yang suggested they spend the night near the city and come see him first thing in the morning; this way he'd have the time to study, analyze, and give this rare affliction his total attention. He had friends who would put the two of them up in a very restful home-style atmosphere, a garage loft just outside of town. Madonna was very grateful for the doctor's concern and graciously accepted.

At 8:00 the next morning, after a quick bite to eat, they were back at Dr. Yang's office. Madonna didn't feel much like eating, and you know about Sammy. Dr. Yang had several types of herbs mixed and measured in sealed bottles with instructions regarding how to administer them. What he had to say next was really unusual; he told Madonna that Sammy also had a mental problem along with this illness. It probably had something to do with his father abandoning him. He told her to do whatever was possible to bring him out of this mental state.

"It seems," said the doctor, "that this rare disease feeds on depression; get rid of the depression and usually the disease is healed." He wished them the best and told Madonna to call him for any reason. The doctor called them a taxi. Madonna thanked him for everything, and off they went to the airport.

The flight back home seemed endless; finally they were back in their Ocean City home. The winter blitz that hit New Jersey had not let up; it was still very cold. During this time, with Sammy being ill, Madonna had taken the time to learn of the Kite Man's background and who really was. She hadn't mentioned this to Sammy because of his condition and really, what did it matter? To her son, he was just the Kite Man.

She wanted to do whatever she could to help her son get out of this depressed state, so she asked Sammy if there was anything she could do for him. He told his Mother that he'd love to have a kite like the Falcon kite; he said that would make him the happiest person in the world. Madonna turned her head away from Sammy so he couldn't see the expression on her face but promised to do what she could.

Madonna, now knowing who Franklin was and his life style change, didn't know if she wanted to approach the man, for she had realized that he'd lost his fortune due to his love for her. To ask him for something that meant so much to him would be very, very hard. However, to save her son's life, she would do anything. Madonna's mother had come to her home to help care for Sammy so she knew he was in safe hands. This enabled her to search out Franklin Armello. She found out where Franklin lived and called a taxi take her into the low-income district.

She knocked on Franklin's door. When Franklin answered, he was awestruck; he couldn't believe what he was seeing. He rubbed his eyes several times to make sure he wasn't dreaming. He turned away slightly embarrassed, she touched his arm and asked if she could come inside.

Once again mixed emotions from the bench crowd: "Don't let her in! Are you nuts?" So protested the majority, believing Franklin shouldn't allow her inside.

Even though Madonna knew Franklin at one time was in love with her, she formally introduced herself, then proceeded to tell him how she had heard of him as the Kite Man. She explained apologetically that she in no way meant to hurt or snub him when that situation transpired years ago and hoped he'd understand. She said that literally thousands of fanatical fans tried to approach her in one way or another.

Franklin said he understood fully and didn't harbor any grudges or malcontent. She then continued that she had a specific reason for coming to see him. He asked her to hold the thought as he wanted to warm the fire.

Franklin's apartment, though in a poor neighborhood, had a unique feature; it contained a working fireplace. Thank goodness for that, because with him struggling, he was still able to get free heat from fallen and dead trees the city removed, and also from scraps of wood he found along the beach.

However, at this time, with the severity of the winter, there was no more wood outside of Franklin's apartment to put in his fireplace. Out of his kindness and consideration for Madonna, he decided he would burn his prized Falcon kite; he could always make another.

In the meantime, Madonna was looking around the apartment at photos of Franklin's past, plus photos people on the beach had taken of his kites, including a beautiful photo of the Falcon. She told him the fire felt good.

He'd managed to afford a phone; dialing the number, he ordered out for pizza from the place where he was employed. For the next few minutes, they made small talk, recalling how each of them had gotten to their unique position in life. Finally the pizza arrived, so they dined by the fire. Franklin then asked her reason for coming to see him.

Madonna replied that her son was extremely ill and could possibly die and that all the doctors were stymied, to say the least. Only one doctor, an herbalist, Dr. Yang thought there was hope. After describing his prognosis, she asked Franklin about his prized Falcon kite, as that was her son's one wish. Franklin's face became expressionless.

Apologizing, he said that very kite was keeping them warm. He told Madonna not to despair, that he would build a special kite for Sammy as good as or better than the Falcon. Never once did he ask Madonna for help or money. Madonna was touched at his kind-hearted, unselfish gesture. She thanked him, then surprised Franklin, telling him that she would supply whatever he needed to build the kite. They finished the pizza; Franklin called a taxi for her and Madonna retuned home. It was a wonderful visit and both of them felt very deep feelings towards the other.

Upon his mother's returning, Sammy asked her if she had the Falcon; she replied that she did not. Sammy's face immediately drooped. Before he could take another breath, she told him how Franklin had burned the kite to keep them warm during her visit but promised to build him a kite as good as or better; Sammy seemed satisfied.

Being good to his word, Franklin built a magnificent kite that looked just like a golden eagle. He delivered the kite to Sammy within a few days. It was so realistic that it looked as if it could fly on its own. It had all of the features of the Falcon, plus with a wingspan of seven feet and length of nine feet, it would have actually dwarfed the Falcon. Franklin named the kite "Sammy II's Golden Eagle."

Sammy recovered within weeks and was back at school in time for the spring session. Every weekend, he stood beside Franklin on the beach, flying his Eagle. Franklin made sure he never built or flew a kite that was bigger than Sammy's.

"Am I seeing a few tears, fellas? Nah, I didn't think so; you're just squinting from the sun. "

So what do we have in the making here, a fairy tale ending? Madonna and Franklin hit it off from the first time they laid eyes on each other at Franklin's apartment. They began to see a lot of one another and fell deeply in love. After a time, the couple became a popular item in Ocean City. Boardwalk businesses and restaurants loved when this fashionable couple graced their premises. By now Franklin had his own legitimate business funded by his fiancée, "Kite Man Enterprises."

"Yeah, that's right, guys, legitimate, so quit your gripin'!"

His famous kites were now sold all over the world and he had two locations on the boardwalk. Madonna met with her attorney about marrying Franklin Armello. Everything seemed to be in order; her divorce to her first husband was final and she had legal custody of Sammy, so why not? Ocean City, New Jersey was a well kept secret for years, but with this extravagant wedding of two famous personalities, the city hit the spotlight. Yes, Madonna Temptation was still a sought after item, and Franklin Armello had made a complete turn around. Oh, and they made great parents for Sammy.

"Just a minute fellas, my cell phone is ringing. Yeah, Mom, this is Sammy; sure, I'll meet you for

lunch. Can I bring my bench buddies? They're cool, Mom; don't worry—see you in about twenty minutes."

One of the guys spoke out: " You're Sammy Armello; we're going to lunch with Madonna Temptation Armello?"

I'd forgotten to mention when Madonna spoke with her attorney, she also had my last name changed to Armello. Come on, I love that guy!

"That's right, guys, Mack and Manco* pizza for lunch; it's my treat!"

*Mack and Manco is a famous delicious pizza made and sold only in Ocean City, New Jersey.

Love Conquers All

This story will take you to an ancient temple deep in the jungles of India. What begins as a summer break and expedition for Will and his father turns into the adventure of a lifetime. Also included in this story, from the *Srimad Bhagavatam* (an ancient Vedic scripture), is the legendary pastime of Lord Nashringhadeva. (Na-shringa-dave)

Love: how does one define the word? Some say it's a verb, some a noun. I say it's from the heart. Almost all mythology and legends have gods or goddesses of love. Over the ages, people have clamored for the feeling of love. Love makes us happy; it makes us feel warm, cozy, satisfied, and fulfilled. When one has lost that loving feeling (as the Righteous Brothers sang in the early 1960's), "It's gone, gone, gone!" People and animals will go to great length to recover that loss; let's see what happens with twelve-and-a-half-year-old Will and his father on their most unusual journey.

Will's father, Dodge Harrison, an archeologist, was sent on assignment in a jungle near Mayapur,

India, where he was to decipher the writings on and in an ancient temple and its cave tunnels beneath. Will's father was able to interpret several ancient languages. He was often sent to mysterious and wonderful places, something he enjoyed immensely. Will was on summer break for this particular trip so he was able to accompany his dad on this several-month journey. Mom said she would rather stay at home and hear about the adventure when they returned.

Now this ancient temple was located deep in the jungle the locals nicknamed Harunya's (Ha-run-ya) hideout, supposedly his palace, until his untimely confrontation. The name referred to a mythological demon who was one of the most hideous ever. The temple was now named after the home of Harunya's conqueror; it was called the Temple of Nashringha. This temple was unbelievably beautiful with great columns and relief's hand carved by artisans of long ago. These carvings depicted gods and demi-gods along with their servants or vessels of travel, be it a chariot or some mysterious, strange-looking beast or animal. It also had the carvings of the half-man, half-lion god Nashringha and his pastimes with the demon Harunya. Each carving or relief told a story or pastime of the figure carved into the surface.

The carvings of Nashringha and Harunya were quite violent and somewhat frightening. The temple priest told Will and his father that even though those particular carvings were frightful, there was a happy ending that actually involved a young child named Prahlad (Pra-lod).

The temple almost seemed out of place in the middle of a hot sweltering jungle. The temple was unusual in that it had a very deep basement area one hundred fifty five feet below the surface of the jungle. They had to have a temporary elevator system installed just to reach the bottom. They were so deep in the jungle that they had to make the elevator operate with ropes, pulleys, and levers.

Along with the supplies was a diesel generator; however, it was only powerful enough to run the lighting they needed and nothing more. Besides, diesel fuel was not available, so they had to be very frugal with the supply they brought with them, all the more reason to hand operate the elevator.

The deep basement had several rooms that led to many uncharted tunnels some which ran all the way back to the city; some were so long and mysterious, they'd never been explored. The writings Will's dad had to decipher and translate were supposedly scattered throughout these many tunnels; Will excitedly hoped they would have to enter those that were unexplored. There were tales of mystic yogis who came to these tunnels go into mystic trance and transport themselves to different parts of India; some said anywhere in the universe!

The priest told how it was done. Long ago, these yogis could meditate for years, slowing their breathing, living on only what matter came in with the air they breathed. When they finally reached Nirvana, a kind of perfection, they would transport themselves anywhere! All this made the trip more exciting for Will; heck, this was more exciting than a baseball fantasy camp or a trip to Disney World!

Now Will and his dad had to prepare for their journey. In Mayapur, Will's dad had hired two knowledgeable and reliable guides who spoke some English and could also help translate the writings. He had also bought other supplies along with the aforementioned generator. They packed everything they needed and went to supper. This was the night before they were to begin; in order to sanctify the journey, which the temple priest felt was necessary, he offered them an evening meal that was blessed before the temple deities, one of those deities being the half-man, half-lion Nashringha.

The meal was not served on traditional plates, but dried banana leaves. The priest and guides ate with the fingers of their right hand; Will's dad managed to find a couple of plastic forks in their supplies. Will noticed that the interior of the temple was just as beautiful as the outside; it was also extremely clean. In fact the marble floor was clean enough to eat off of, and so they did.

When the meal was almost over, Will asked the temple priest, whose name he learned was Kashi, (Ka-she) if he could tell the story of the half-man, half-lion god. From what the priest told him, and the carvings on the temple, the deity on the altar had really whet his curiosity. The priest said after he cleaned up from their meal he would gladly tell the pastime of Harunya Kasipu (Ka-she-pu) and Lord Nashringhadeva. Will was so excited he offered to help.

The guides always enjoyed hearing this pastime

so they went outside and in a clearing in front of the temple built a campfire. Everyone sat cross-legged on blankets around the fire on this cool, clear evening as the priest started to tell the story.

Kashi began in a soft voice: "Long, long ago the demon Harunya Kasipu wanted to become immortal; he wanted a benediction that he could not be killed. He began an extreme meditation and sacrifice to the demigod Lord Brahma, (Bra-ma) lord of the universe. He stood on one leg and did not eat or drink anything for hundreds of years. In fact, he stood in one spot for so long, buzzards had picked away his flesh and ants devoured the lower part of his body; he was basically a living skeleton." Will, his father and the guides sat mesmerized as they intently listened by the glowing fire.

Kashi continued, "Finally Lord Brahma appeared before him and said, 'Harunya Kasipu, you are without a doubt one of the most feared demons in the material world; however, your devoted meditation to me must not go unanswered. How may I serve you?'"

"Harunya Kasipu responded, 'I want to be immortal!'"

"Lord Brahma replied, 'I cannot offer you that boon, for even I am not immortal and must answer to the ravages of time.'"

"Harunya thought for a moment, then began; 'I do not want to be killed by any human or animal, nor do I want to be killed in the day or night time. I do not want to be killed in the sky, on the land, or in the water, nor do I want to be killed indoors or out and I shall not be killed by any weapon. I also want to remain as a young man.'"

"In this way Harunya Kasipu felt confident that if Lord Brahma granted this benediction he would basically be immortal."

"Lord Brahma could not refuse this request. 'I will grant you this benediction, Harunya Kasipu, heaven help your soul.' Lord Brahma ascended towards the heavens and in seconds was gone."

"Harunya Kasipu was a true demon; he spread fear across the universe. While doing so, he managed to create a son with one of his many consorts; his son's name was Prahlad. When Prahlad was old enough Harunya took the boy by his side and wanted to educate him in his demonic ways; there was a problem, however. Prahlad had no interest in being a demon; he just wanted to worship his Lord, lord Nashringhadeva. After repeatedly trying to convert him, Harunya grew impatient with his spiritual son and began to threaten him, which did not work; Prahlad would not budge from his dedication. This was driving Harunya Kasipu mad, insane; he had to get rid of the boy—he was a nuisance!"

"'I will poison the boy,' Harunya thought. He made up a concoction of poisonous herbs and handed it to Prahlad to drink. Now Prahlad was no dummy; he knew what his father was up to, so he took the drink and swallowed all of it. While doing so he meditated on his Lord, confident that he would be protected."

"When he did not die, Harunya Kasipu became

even more furious; he placed his son in a den of snakes, and again it did not faze Prahlad and he survived. Harunya Kasipu could take this no more he climbed with his son to the top of the highest mountain in the universe and pushed him off."

"He said, 'Now I know he is finished; so much for the boy and his Lord!' He headed back to his palace, thinking the ordeal with his disrespectful son was over. When he returned, Prahlad was standing there meditating on his Lord. This was it for Harunya Kasipu; he lost his composure and went into a ranting rage."

"'Where is your Lord? I don't see him; is he over here?'"

"He broke down the door leading to the royal bath. 'Is he up there?' he said, pointing towards the ceiling. It was about dusk, close to sunset, when this was all taking place."

"Finally, in one last fit of rage, he screamed, 'Is he in these columns?' As he said this, he lunged at the columns, bursting them in two. Suddenly, there was a gigantic unbearable roar; it was so loud it shook the entire universe. Out of those very columns appeared Lord Nashringhadeva, a fearful roaring half-man, half-lion beast!"

"He grabbed Harunya Kasipu and laid him across his lap and bifurcated him with his long sharp lion-nails, killing him instantly! He came through the column, which placed him neither inside or out; being dusk, it was neither day or night; sitting him on his lap Harunya was not killed in the sky, land, or water."

"During all of this, Prahlad was not afraid; in fact, upon seeing his Lord's fearful form, he loved him even more. Prahlad's Lord had beaten his demon father at his own game. Prahlad became a personal servant of Lord Nashringha; as legend goes, he is still doing so today."

The fire had become nothing more than glowing embers; a chill was now in the night air. It was time to turn in; everyone had to get an early start tomorrow. Will was so excited from that amazing story and the adventure he was about to begin that he could hardly close his eyes.

Will's father woke him early the next day before sunrise; the air was still cool and the jungle was fairly quiet as all the entities of the jungle had not come out of their evening slumber. They ate a simple breakfast with the guides, loaded their gear on their backs, and headed through the temple towards the elevator that was in a room in the back. Kashi the priest, who had been awake since 4:00 a.m., waited by the elevator to offer his blessing, wish them luck and a safe journey, then lower them down to the main basement room. Now what Will was finally waiting for would take place.

"Let the fun begin," he thought to himself; he grabbed his Dad's arm as the priest lowered them down. It was extremely dark; once they were lowered into the huge room, the generator was only able to light the elevator shaft to the basement. Everyone had been issued a miner's hard hat with a powerful lamp attached to the front.

Dodge gave some pertinent instructions: "All

right, everyone, it's time to get serious. Most importantly, use the buddy system; stay close to your partner. Second, do not in any way disfigure or damage the writings or anything else you see down here! Stay honest; anyone caught destroying or trying to pilfer will be immediately dismissed without compensation! Is that clear?"

"Let's try to have fun and learn something new about this glorious, mysterious, and intriguing civilization. We have enough supplies to stay down here for three days; use them sensibly, and use your walkie-talkie transmitter if you are lost. However, it may not work in all situations. I don't expect we'll be that far apart most of the time anyway. Are there any questions?" The guides nor Will could think of any; besides, Will just wanted to get going.

Will's dad took out a small pad and pencil and began to map out their direction so hopefully they could find their way back. It seemed to Will as they headed into the tunnels that the further they went, the more they descended. In the first hour and twenty minutes, they covered approximately two miles into the first tunnel and it seemed uneventful. Most of what was written on the tunnel sides were common prayers and meditations seen on the surface. Suddenly the main tunnel split into four separate tunnels; Harrison and the guides started searching the walls for possible instruction or directions for entering the tunnels. However, there were none.

The guides search the tunnels

"What are we going to do now, Dad?" Harrison thought for a moment, then went into his supplies and brought out three more tablets with pencils, plus something no one, not even Will knew about—digital cameras!

"Time for a change of plans," he said. "In order to get the most out of our time down here, I think we should split up."

"Me too, Dad?"

"Yes, Will, I trust you and believe I have a pretty safe foolproof idea." He handed out the pads and pencils along with the cameras.

"All of us will walk no more than thirty minutes

into the tunnels; mark down anything that will serve as a landmark or guide post. If you see anything of interest, take a picture, so when we go back we will know what to look for. This will also help if you can't understand or find what you've written on your pads. I must stress that you keep the camera use to a minimum; there are no spare batteries for these cameras." Dodge quickly thought to himself how foolish it was not to bring any spare batteries, for the cameras, walkie talkies, even the helmets—geez! He told himself he would not let that happen in the future—a lot of good that would do now!

"Keep your walkie talkies on during this time; we still may be able to communicate with each other." Will and his dad would take the two inside tunnels; the guides would take the outside two.

"It's ten thirty a.m.; everyone make sure you're back at this spot by eleven thirty a.m.!" Will hugged his dad and off he went into the tunnel, just like a grown-up archeologist; he was a little scared but felt proud that his dad trusted him.

Will had been more than slightly interested in his dad's work at home, so he was very comfortable with the situation between him and his dad. Will was, after all, a very bright young man; by working and studying with his dad at home, he could read and translate some of the ancient languages his dad had to translate and decipher. One of those languages was Sanskrit, which was the main language in these tunnels. His dad had encouraged Will to see if he could decipher any symbols on his own. Now heading into his own tunnel, Will was ecstatic, a chance to try on his own.

The tunnel Will traveled seemed different than the first long one; it seemed to have a light of its own, a soft violet glow. Will was about twenty minutes into his journey when finally he came upon some symbols. They were the most beautifully-written symbols he had ever seen; running his hand over the impressions, they really did seem mystical. Nervously he spoke out loud as he began to translate roughly.

"Where ever you want to go, by your thoughts to and fro, to the end of the universe, places you have never seen, to the heavens, planets and galaxies, everywhere in between!" Now there was something really unusual. At the end of the writing was a place where you placed the first three fingers of your right hand.

Will was curious; what could it hurt to place your fingers there? This tunnel hasn't been used for centuries. Will placed his fingers properly and read the writing again; in an instant Will was gone! After about an hour, at eleven thirty, the two guides and Harrison appeared out of their tunnels back into the main one. Harrison was anxious as to why Will hadn't returned; he waited about five minutes, then tried to call Will on the walkie-talkie: no response, just static. He met with the guides and hurriedly decided to look for Will.

The three of them cautiously entered the tunnel; in a few minutes, they also saw the violet glow.

Slowly they moved through the tunnel, checking every nook and cranny, looking at anything that looked like writing. When they reached the spot where Will last was, they saw his pencil, writing tablet, walkie-talkie and the camera. Harrison saw the beautiful writing, translated it, saw the finger holes, and began to wonder. Could it be? Was Will able to translate and read this writing? Harrison told the guides to stay at the spot even if he disappeared; he read the symbols, placed his hand in the proper position; he too was gone!

Will didn't quite know what happened at first. After coming to his senses, he realized he was no longer in the tunnels under the jungle, but on the Moon! He was scared and confused but did not panic.

"There must be a solution to this," he thought. Though totally absorbed in his situation, he managed to look out and see Earth.

"How unbelievably beautiful; if I only hadn't dropped the camera!" Words couldn't describe what he saw; he felt like an astronaut without a space suit.

"Wait a minute! How am I breathing? Better yet, how am I even alive?" Without thinking, he bent down and grabbed a handful of moon soil; it was soft and silky. Will wondered if the soil felt that way because of the high silicone content. Anyway, back to the immediate situation.

Of all the places he could have come to, how did he get on to the moon? He thought and thought, then realized the last thing he watched before starting on this trip was a story on the History Channel about colonization of the moon. His own thoughts had brought him here.

"This is really bizarre but kind of cool," he pondered. He realized he wasn't cold or uncomfortable in any way, just standing on an ocean of glowing sand, on an object he had observed many times from Earth. He remembered when he'd look up at the moon how beautiful it looked, definitely unreachable to most earthlings, yet here he was standing on its surface! Seemingly hours passed. During this time, he used the moon's one-sixth gravity to travel most of the lighted half.

One thing that bothered him was all the space trash previous astronauts had left behind. "We even litter on the moon!"

He began thinking in earnest; would he ever see his dad, mom, family, or friends again? Even more disconcerting, would he ever get back to Earth? How did that translation go?

"Oh yeah," he remembered, and said the mantra to himself; he placed the three fingers of both hands against each other.

"What the heck, I gotta try something." In an instant, he was back in the tunnel, his dad by his side, both of them laughing and sobbing at the same time. He hugged his dad for what seemed like forever. The guides were jumping up and down, calling out like school children. Not only were they glad to see the father and his son, but they realized that their ancient legends now had some truth to them. The tunnels seemed to echo with joyous energy. They decided to head back to the surface; the guides told them they'd been gone for almost three days.

Once back on the surface, they bathed, put on fresh clothes, and went to dinner. Kashi the temple priest had prepared a feast in their honor, for he was amazed at what had transpired down in the tunnels. Will's dad told them he also had traveled throughout the universe searching for his beloved son. Somehow he was able to transport himself to many different places, but he was having no luck. Finally on what he thought was Jupiter, Harrison had become absolutely desperate.

He thought of how he loved his son and enjoyed his company especially on this trip; he thought of how they'd bonded on a much deeper level. He thought if they were together again, they'd be not only father and son but close friends for life.

"Completely opposite of Harunya Kasipu and his son Prahlad!" He thought of how fortunate he was to be able to father a child and how Will was a special gift to him and his wife. With those thoughts in mind, he momentarily closed his eyes; upon opening them, he found that Will was there before him. They were back in the tunnel; love had brought him back together with his son.

After resting for a couple of days, recalling the journey again and again, each time remembering something they hadn't mentioned before, everyone agreed it was time to go back down in the tunnels to continue their work. They continued their work for another two months, traveling deeper into the tunnels than anyone had ever done. They found, deciphered, and translated many more writings. Some were meaningful, others beautiful and poetic; however, none could compare to the writing Will had translated that first day in his tunnel. And yes, they did get many pictures, including one of the writing that took Will and his father on their unbelievable trek.

Finally, with summer coming to an end, Will and his dad were tired yet elated with this unusual experience. Dodge paid and thanked the guides for their help; he thanked the priest for his hospitality. He donated the generator, cameras, and what supplies were left to the temple. They left the jungle and traveled back to Mayapur. Once at the airport, they boarded their chartered plane and headed anxiously for home looking forward to familiar surroundings, family and friends.

The moral to this amazing tale is this: Love is more powerful than any mysticism or trance. Love conquers all!

The Secret of the Lost City Women

For the most part this is a world dominated by the power of man. This is unusual in that there are over twice as many women as men on the planet; here is a tale where the women have total power and control. We have the stories and legends of the lost continent of Atlantis and more recently the lost continent of Lemuria. Lemuria was a civilization similar to Atlantis. All of us have heard of or witnessed about alien spacecraft from the unknown. Now enjoy a modern legend of a lost city that is here on earth, and about the power and determination of these special women.

There is a river that flows to the sea somewhere near the equator that folks say isn't always there. This river flows to the edge of a mountain that is made of precious stones: emeralds, amethyst, diamonds, and rubies that are exposed on every side. Mount Atmospheris, as it is aptly called, is so high that when the river tumbles from its edge, it creates a magnificent waterfall, a waterfall so high that it seems to tumble from the heavens. The waterfall evaporates to a mist before touching the sea. When sunlight or moonlight reflects off the exposed jewels, combined with the heavy mist, this creates a mesmerizing effect that attracts all who witness the sight. Under this mist at the base of the mountain are two beautifully-carved solid gates that are the entrance to this lost city.

The Entrance to the Lost City

As with the continent of Atlantis, many are said to enter but do not return.

The description of this city is of mythological proportions. Once you dock your boat or ship at the gates, you then enter onto a golden walkway. Orchards of every kind of fruit and nut surround you; they stretch for miles and miles as far as the eye can see. Any kind of fruit imaginable, domestic or exotic, can been seen growing in these well-manicured orchards.

Once past the orchards, you then enter the flower and vegetable gardens, again as neat and well kept as anyone could imagine. The sight and scents are overwhelming as you are in the perfect garden. Vegetables grow with dramatic flower arrangements planted amongst them. The color of this place makes it so you don't know where to turn or look next, not that it matters, as everything is outrageously beautiful. You feel as if you have been intoxicated, yet you haven't ingested anything liquid or solid; the multiple aromas have you reeling in delight.

To this point, you have not seen any type of building or piece of machinery. Finally, the gardens end and you come to the outskirts of the city, and again you are taken aback. Wonderfully-designed homes appear, every one different from the other, yet in perfect harmony, a neighborhood where anyone would love to reside. Tree-lined streets give just enough shade to keep the homes cool, yet allow enough light for flowers to grow on the well-maintained grounds; everything is impeccably clean. Traveling though this suburbia, you notice that there must be varied levels of importance, as all homes and properties vary in size. As if in a dream, you come to a crest in the horizon and there before you exists a city to behold.

Here is a city to set the example for all cities.

Again, every building is coordinated with the others; it is very pleasing to look upon. The streets are well-organized, so when going from place to place, you never become confused or lost. The street signs are large and easy to read, and they are also color-coded by direction east, west etc., so you know where you are at all times. No need for a Global Mapping System here!

In the evening, every area of the city is evenly lighted and there are noticeably no gaudy advertising billboards to distract from the city's opulence. The city is not without its amenities, however; there are well-maintained and decorated parks throughout. You are able to frequent these parks any time of day or night, as the city is crime-free. Shopping is a pleasure, with neatly-kept stores with every variety of item available, plus there is always a sale! Entertainment and dining is of the utmost importance. There are theaters and movie complexes everywhere; dining is available in every ethnic variety. There are also night clubs with dancing and music of every style. Yes, there are vehicles in this city, mostly public transportation, but you can't hear them, for they are powered by solar energy that will work even after the sun has set.

Who has done this, you say? Well, hang on a moment.

Obvious throughout every aspect of this journey is that you see mostly, you guessed it, women. At first glance, you would almost think the population is entirely women. However, this is not a fact. This civilization is indeed run by women; the grand part of this civilization is that, unlike in most stories or as we see on television, these women are not "perfect" specimens. Yes, they are extremely healthy and live long productive lives, but they accept one another for who they are. I'll bet you were expecting perfect Amazon-type ladies with picture-perfect figures and looks; sorry, that's not the real world. These are amazing ladies inside and out, of all sizes and age, living in perfect harmony with each other.

Not that these ladies are not attractive; indeed they are! These ladies possess a quality that has taken many years to develop; we could all learn by their example.

It is a known fact that men who have been at sea for long periods of time enjoy the company of a woman. It has been said that some men of the sea actually went looking for this place, although most have discovered it by accident. Legend has it when these women were in need of men, they let the gates be slightly askew, allowing the alluring scent of their abode to drift out onto the open sea. You see, there are no homegrown men in this special place; it seems they are all imported. Now, at a closer look, yes, we do see men definitely the minority. Looking at these fellows they do seem to be happy, content, satisfied.

Is that a glazed look I see in their eyes? No, I'm just kidding.

The men are genuinely fulfilled in every aspect of their lives.

Here's how it all takes place; the leaders of this society learned long ago that they were better off acquiring the opposite sex in this manner. In a recent interview with their leader, the honorable Governess Jalena, who by the way has doctorates in sociology and psychology, we acquired this information about the lost city.

Governess Jalena, why do you, for the lack of a better word, capture your males in this way?

"We do not capture our men sir, how dare you ask such a question! No man is kept here if that is not his desire. As you say, men at sea often desire the company of a woman. Only when we sense that these men have that desire do we invite them to see if they'd like to settle into our paradise."

I see, please continue.

"Many, many years ago, our society was rescued by the Roman goddess Juno; she is the goddess of marriage and childbirth, the protector of married women, and queen of the gods. Before she came to help us, there were men present; these men were an offspring of the god of the underworld, Pluto. These were mean and hateful men; they took advantage of our kind and loving nature. We were virtually slaves in their presence, and then Juno came along. She protected us by banishing these men where they belonged, back to the underworld."

Still you do not have men of your own. What is the reason for this?

"Until that time, our city was present on the planet on an island just off the northern coast of South America. When Juno came to us, we were a very frightened group; years of ridicule and strife had taken their toll. She felt it would be best if we were hidden from the rest of the world, our entrance covered by the great waterfall, only appearing when we were in need of the male gender. Goddess Juno gave us great intelligence and strength so we would be able to maintain a city of our own. She said we should only attract desirable men as needed."

Does your city have a name? Please explain the process you have put in place.

"In her honor, our city is named Juno. As you know, most of our men are sailors, merchant marines, or sea-loving gentlemen; sometimes getting them to stay can be difficult. We offer them every amenity available in our city plus any woman they are attracted to as long as the feeling is mutual. If they have the desire to stay with their partner, we ask them to marry. Anyone who marries must have a family."

Wouldn't having children give at least a fifty-fifty chance of having a male child?

"No. Due to our terrible experience, Juno asked the god Jupiter to make it so we can only bear female children. In this way we are able to keep this a female-dominated society."

So the men are actually here by their own choosing.

"Yes, and we are grateful; they are allowed to live out their days in peace and happiness."

One last question, how do you avoid jealously, discrimination, war?

"That's easy; we either have a bake sale or go shopping! Seriously, we take great pride in our form of government and have a commitment of total peace, always. This ethic has been handed down from generation to generation."

Thank you for your time and kindness, Governess.

"You are quite welcome."

An unusual tale, to say the least—naturally Governess Jalena would not give out her e-mail address or the location of her lost city we now know as Juno.

It has been said that if you do leave the lost city, you are never quite the same. Life takes on a whole new and different perspective; it is a very positive experience. The cleanliness, awesome beauty, fragrant aromas, the feeling of safety and security always stay with you.

One can only hope that someday the rest of the planet will follow the lost city of Juno's ideals. As long as people are greedy, hungry for power, maintain religious differences, and continue racial indifference, there is not much hope. Maybe that is another reason why Governess Jalena keeps her paradise a secret. Good for her—at least someone has the right idea. Maybe we do need a woman for president. Hey, it's a start.

A letter from Governess Galena:

Dear Citizens of the Planet,
Are you satisfied with the conditions

in which you are living? Does it make you sad to pick up the newspaper, turn on the television, or look on the internet and see hatred, crime, poverty and injustice? There is an answer, but the time is now; you must make the change while there is still hope.

Obviously you cannot count on your governments to do that which is needful; they are too locked into big business and it would not be profitable for them to make a drastic change. It is quite a dilemma; each and every one of you must take charge. How you must do this is as individuals creating a massive whole that cannot be ignored. It will not be easy. This does not mean a march on your capital or a parade through the streets.

You must do this at home; here is my suggestion.

I understand the way things are today, that usually both parents must work, so you don't have much time to spend with your children. That is OK; you must lead by example. I'm not going to waste your time about diet or living preferences; however, whatever you do must be with the highest standard and result in mind. Treat everything and everyone as you would wish to be treated. Do not mock or ridicule someone because of color, religion, or defect. Respect people of all ages, especially older citizens, as you can learn much from them. Do not harbor grudges or speak ill of someone when not in his or her presence. In our city, if we must say something good or bad, we say it right to the person intended in the most honorable and respectful way possible.

Practice cleanliness in every aspect of your life. Keep your home, property, yourself, and family neat and clean. Learn to recycle, no matter how useless it seems. Everyone who recycles will help save the planet. Do not litter! Littering shows you do not have respect for your planet or your fellow citizens. The planet is a beautiful place; it is a privilege to live here, and littering only defaces nature's wonderful gift.

Replace hate, greed and hostility with love and compassion. Good things will come about if we change our attitude; we will override the evil thinkers of this world. I know this may sound like an impossible task but even if you attempt a few of these suggestions it will make a difference, for you and the planet.

With all hope and love;
Governess Jalena

Sure, lots of people say they're musicians, but talk is cheap; it takes practice and dedication. Finding the "right" mix of talent is not so easy. This story tells of a group of guys who came together and worked very hard for:

The Performance

I'll never forget how it all started. My name is Vontarie Donner; I play acoustic and electric guitar. I've been playing since I was thirteen years old. Many musicians and teachers would say I got a bit of a late start, that I'm not the perfect protégé player. To them, I say well, never mind what I say; it doesn't matter. Tal Farlow, a famous jazz guitarist, didn't start playing until he was twenty one! I've worked and practiced very hard; besides, I'm the one with the fantastic story to tell.

Did you ever want something so bad you could taste it? I don't mean pizza or tacos, either; I mean the desire to accomplish something most people only dream about. It all started about five years ago in my garage in a small town called Tullahoma. I'd been playing about 6 years and I was ready to get together with other musicians to start a band that played original music. None of that cover music for me, or "Top Forty" as my dad called it. My dad is a percussionist, drums mostly; he played full time and was on the road for years in his younger days.

I began going to the pawn shop and music store in town to try to find musicians who would be interested in doing the same thing. Pawn shops are a great place to find musicians; they're always hocking, selling, or trying to get a good deal on an instrument some other poor soul had to sell to survive. Thank goodness, so far I haven't found myself in the latter position, although I've gotten a couple great deals on "axes" for myself. In a small town, the talent pool isn't that great and most of the established players usually stick together; it's very hard to get in with these people. The word clique comes to mind, clique meaning basically someone has to move away or pass on to the next life for anyone to join their group.

Eventually I did find one pretty good musician, a bassist named Dave. It's funny; every time I mention that name to Dad, he says, "Is Dave in?" I don't know, it must be some kind of sixties thing. Then one day when I was about to expand my search area to some surrounding towns, I met a guy who delivers pizzas at the local Pizza Hut. He is a guitarist who can sing and has the same passion as me; his name is Rob.

Now I was getting somewhere; the next thing we had to do was see if we could play together. I arranged for us to jam at my garage one evening so we could play and see if we were compatible. Dad had told me stories of how you could have the greatest musicians, but if everybody's head isn't screwed on right, it's not going to happen. He told me that was probably the biggest pitfall. I tend to agree; I see a lot of professionals break up their band in its prime—ego, I guess.

Our first practice session together was OK, not the greatest but passable. It seemed like it took an hour for us to get in tune.

Dad told me, "Get used to it! Sometimes I sat at my drums so long my butt would fall asleep!" Thanks, Dad, that's a little more information than I needed to know. When we finally played, it sounded, as I said, OK, definitely worth getting together for another session. I have enough sense to know you can't make a judgment the first time in music unless everyone clicks; I don't mean the same meaning as the other clique.

In the meantime, I had to try to find a keyboard

player and a drummer. I know what you're thinking, but that's a last resort.

The next time we got together for practice, I asked Rob and Dave if they knew of a keyboard player or drummer: "Yeah, Dad, Dave's in!"

They didn't know of anyone outside of the guys in the clique. Both of them suggested you-know-who on drums too: "You guys play a complete song and I'll sit in!" What a prima-donna!

"OK, Dad, we'll let you know."

"No, I'll let you know!" he responded. This practice sounded a lot better than the first; Dad thought he recognized a song.

In these first practices, we were playing standard songs; this way we could get a sound without having to learn each other's music at the same time, which will come later. I told the guys we'd have to expand our search for other musicians to the surrounding towns. We decided that on a Saturday before Rob and I had to go to work, we'd drive to the towns of Manchester, Winchester, and Shelbyville to ask around. We didn't know if we'd make all the stops in one morning, but that was our plan.

Nine a.m. Saturday, we met at Rob's apartment, hopped into my old GMC Suburban, and off we went, first stop Winchester, as that was the closest town. Our plan was music stores, pawn shops and coffee shops. The coffee shop was for us; at this early hour, we had hold our eyes open with toothpicks.

Winchester was a bust; anybody we met said, "We're only into country music, dudes." We stopped for our third cup of coffee; everyone seemed to be talking faster. Rob suggested we try Manchester next; there was a big pawn shop right off the interstate.

"We only have time for one more town anyway," he said. Dave, who is very quiet, a trait of most bassists, finally spoke.

"Maybe being near the interstate there will be a better chance of meeting a keyboard player and drummer." Rob and I both agreed and off we drove towards Manchester.

When we arrived in Manchester, we decided to go to the pawn shop first; the music store on the square was only a "hole in the wall" anyway. Wow, this was a nice-size pawn shop; the music room was as big as the whole pawn shop in Tullahoma. It was around ten-thirty, quarter to eleven, so there were lots of people milling around the music room, and hopefully some were musicians, maybe a keyboardist or drummer.

"OK, guys, spread out and work the room; we only have about an hour, then I've got to go to work," Rob said. What luck—there are a couple of guys looking at keyboards! As if magnetized, we all headed in that direction I held my hand up, signaling Rob and Dave to stay back. We didn't want to scare these people off, and after all the coffee we had, they'd probably think we were on something. I pulled myself together and decided I'd talk with the guy toying with the synthesizer first.

"Hey, how you doing? That's a nice piece of equipment."

The fellow looked at me kind of funny then responded, "No speaky Anglish!" Just like me to pick the wrong person; well let me try this guy.

"Hey, how ya doin'? My name's Von; I play guitar."

"Hey, man, I'm Jeff, I play the keys. Know anybody lookin' for a keyboardist?" I must have looked dumbfounded; I couldn't speak and I think I was pinching myself.

Before I actually could say anything, Rob chimed in and I do mean chimed: "Sure we are! My name's Rob; I play rhythm and sing, and this is our bassist Dave!"

We shook hands, gave high-fives, exchanged cell phone numbers and e-mails and said we looked forward to getting together.

Besides working a part-time job, I was also a full-time college student; Rob was training to become a manager at his job, and Dave also had a full-time job. We didn't know much about Jeff; however, he seemed more than willing to meet our schedule.

Finally, on a Thursday evening, we were able to have our first practice with Jeff. Upon arriving at the garage his first words were, "What, no drummer!"

We told him we'd been looking but with no luck so far; he stated that he didn't know of anyone either as he had just moved to the area.

"Yeah, Dad, Dave's in!'

"What's that all about?" Jeff asked. We all just shrugged and rolled our eyes.

"Von's dad is a musician; we think it must be

es, the jam came to an end with a colossa e ending. A garage ending is when everyon band kind of solos together for some time with eye contact, everyone ends the song er with a tumultuous crash.

first sound spoken was from guess who: , are you guys trying to kill me? I'm old, you " Everyone laughed as we all knew what dad t; it was ecstatic! The jam was inspirational, g, and above all, intensely musical; we knew that point forward our original music was to be just fine.

started doing our original music the very next rsal,; sometimes dad wouldn't join us until orked the chords and vocals, and then he'd with the arrangements. He is very good with ging. It took us about a year to get our toire together; we had enough material for a hour performance.

the end of this one particular rehearsal, dad d, "Well, guys, we've been rehearsing close to r now; it's time to make a move. You've written great songs and we've put together some tanding arrangements; we should step out or might start to lose our momentum. We don't t to get stale; we want to be fresh and intense." fter we packed up our gear, we all went into the ly room to discuss our options.

ob began, "Maybe we can get a few small gigs lly to get a feel of playing in a live situation. We k our music is good but we really haven't gotten feedback from others except our family and ds."

some kind of thing from the sixties. You know how those guys are," Rob stated. Jeff smiled and continued to set up his equipment.

I told Jeff that we should play anyway; if the sound was right, we could probably find a drummer from the area.

Jeff then asked, "What instrument does your dad play?"

We all answered in unison, "Drums."

"Oh," Jeff responded, mildly amused and intrigued. Everyone tuned the instruments much faster and easier, I might add, as a keyboard really helps when it comes to tuning. Jeff suggested the first thing we try together should be a jam. A jam is when you pick a key to play in along with a chord progression and from that point it's just your creativity that comes out as music, so that's what we did, a jam in 'G'.

From the first measure, things just seemed to come together; we all played off of one another and it sounded fantastic. The jam lasted about fifteen minutes before we come to a stop. We were all so into the music no one had noticed my dad step into the garage to listen.

"Now that had some potential, guys; you sounded really good." We were all sweating and winded from such an ecstatic jam; it seemed like we were floating in air.

"Thanks," we all responded, gratified that my hard-core father was moved by our music. We played for another couple of hours doing some old Zeppelin, Deep Purple, and others from the seventies; for hard-core rockers like ourselves, we liked that era's music.

When we finally stepped out of the garage the sun was setting. Rob and Dave lit up a cigarette as Jeff spoke.

"Guys, that was great! What about a drummer? What about your dad? Von, do you think he'd consider playing with us?"

"That would save us from wasting any more time looking and your dad's a really good musician," Rob added.

"I'll ask him," I said, "but no guarantee."

We set our next practice for Saturday evening, packed up our gear, and said our goodbyes. Now came the big question for my dad. Dad was relaxing in his recliner, watching a baseball game; he still had one more ten-hour work day ahead of him, so he was taking it easy. He began to speak as soon as I entered the door.

"You guys sounded pretty good tonight; that Jeff on keyboards really seemed to make a difference."

"Yeah, Dad, it was a great experience for me. Dad, the guys all wanted me to ask you if you would consider sitting in with us during the next rehearsal."

He kind of smiled and responded saying "Are you serious, dude?"

"Sure, you know in music age is not a factor; you've told me that yourself!"

"Well, then, sure, I'll give it a shot, but only if I get to take a drum solo in every song!"

"Yeah, right, Dad," and we both laughed. During

the next couple of days, Dad   minut
cleaning up his drum ro   garag
needed) as our next rehearsal   in the
Actually that was pretty cool w   then
rehearse in an air-conditione   togeth

The guys showed up Saturd   The
I had talked with my father as t   "Wha
of intense drumming comin   know
house.   mean
"I guess he said yes," was the   drivin
I answered, "Only if he can   from
song, that's the deal"   going
Their faces twisted and the   We
"What, is he crazy?"   rehea
"You already know the an   we w
besides, he was only kidding." I   help
their gear into the house that   arra
in the drum room and everyone   repe
Dave blurted, "Air conditionir   two-
entered, Dad stopped playing.   At
"Sounded great," Jeff said; th   state
nodded in agreement. I knew th   a ye
an exciting evening; it seemed l   som
for everyone to set up the equipn   outs
axes in tune. Finally the momen   we
were ready.   wan
"How 'bout a jam in C?" asked   A
Dad set the tempo, "One, two,   fam
down a driving beat and off we we   R
with live drums was an amazing   loca
didn't think five people playing tog   thi
musician could sound so good. Af   any
                                                   frie

"Do you think we should try to get an agent?" I said. My father almost flew out of his recliner.

"An agent, what, are you crazy? They're like bandits with a license! You have to be very careful if you do contact an agent; make sure, check his or her credentials and reputation before talking with them. In the past, my experience with talent agents has been shaky at best, and one was a very good friend. He went under the name of Joe Drift; believe me, there were times we drifted, all right, from one end of the country to the other; plus, some of the establishments we played were pretty shady."

"We wound up calling him 'Snow Drift,' because a lot of the places we played we went into totally blind; sometimes we had to alter our repertoire completely to fit the situation and that's not easy. Although I guess today it's quite possible you could find and check out an agent over the internet, I'm sure there are a lot more possibilities."

Dad always manages to wind up thinking positively and up to date, he passed on experience from his past without being stuck in that past.

Jeff spoke up, "From my experience it's always best to play in front of a live audience; perhaps we can find a hall or something where we can sell tickets and with that money at least recoup our expenses."

Dave said quietly, "What about the Civic Center on Jackson Street?" There was a silence that seemed to last several minutes; everyone seemed to be considering the possiblity.

Finally Rob began, "Everyone is used to events at the Civic Center; they have plays, music and lectures, and maybe we should check into what it would cost to rent it for a night."

"Don't forget that there will be other expenses, such as tickets and advertising," I said.

Dad added, "You would have to pay agent fees and travel money if we had to go out of town, plus the possibility of equipment rental; I believe with the Civic Center that would be all-inclusive. Say we are able to rent the Center a couple of months from now; that would give us inspiration, plus we could start collecting dues that we would use to pay for the extra expenses such as advertising. I think Von's mom and I could help with that part. However, you are going want to see how the Civic Center wants to get paid."

"I don't have to go into work until three in the afternoon Monday and I have no school. I'll stop at the Center and check out the situation," I said.

"I'll go with you; I can meet you there at ten in the morning," Rob added. It was getting late and there wasn't much more we could do, so we set up the next rehearsal, saying we would keep in touch until then.

Rob and I pulled into the Civic Center parking lot at almost the same time; it was a little before ten. We discussed what we would say and walked towards the front entrance. When we got there, a sign was taped on one of the doors: "Please use the side entrance and ring the bell." An arrow was pointing to the left side of the building.

some kind of thing from the sixties. You know how those guys are," Rob stated. Jeff smiled and continued to set up his equipment.

I told Jeff that we should play anyway; if the sound was right, we could probably find a drummer from the area.

Jeff then asked, "What instrument does your dad play?"

We all answered in unison, "Drums."

"Oh," Jeff responded, mildly amused and intrigued. Everyone tuned the instruments much faster and easier, I might add, as a keyboard really helps when it comes to tuning. Jeff suggested the first thing we try together should be a jam. A jam is when you pick a key to play in along with a chord progression and from that point it's just your creativity that comes out as music, so that's what we did, a jam in 'G'.

From the first measure, things just seemed to come together; we all played off of one another and it sounded fantastic. The jam lasted about fifteen minutes before we come to a stop. We were all so into the music no one had noticed my dad step into the garage to listen.

"Now that had some potential, guys; you sounded really good." We were all sweating and winded from such an ecstatic jam; it seemed like we were floating in air.

"Thanks," we all responded, gratified that my hard-core father was moved by our music. We played for another couple of hours doing some old Zeppelin, Deep Purple, and others from the seventies; for hard-core rockers like ourselves, we liked that era's music.

When we finally stepped out of the garage the sun was setting. Rob and Dave lit up a cigarette as Jeff spoke.

"Guys, that was great! What about a drummer? What about your dad? Von, do you think he'd consider playing with us?"

"That would save us from wasting any more time looking and your dad's a really good musician," Rob added.

"I'll ask him," I said, "but no guarantee."

We set our next practice for Saturday evening, packed up our gear, and said our goodbyes. Now came the big question for my dad. Dad was relaxing in his recliner, watching a baseball game; he still had one more ten-hour work day ahead of him, so he was taking it easy. He began to speak as soon as I entered the door.

"You guys sounded pretty good tonight; that Jeff on keyboards really seemed to make a difference."

"Yeah, Dad, it was a great experience for me. Dad, the guys all wanted me to ask you if you would consider sitting in with us during the next rehearsal."

He kind of smiled and responded saying "Are you serious, dude?"

"Sure, you know in music age is not a factor; you've told me that yourself!"

"Well, then, sure, I'll give it a shot, but only if I get to take a drum solo in every song!"

"Yeah, right, Dad," and we both laughed. During

the next couple of days, Dad volunteered me into cleaning up his drum room (no explanation needed) as our next rehearsal would be held there. Actually that was pretty cool with me; we could now rehearse in an air-conditioned environment.

The guys showed up Saturday evening and knew I had talked with my father as they heard the sound of intense drumming coming from inside the house.

"I guess he said yes," was the first thing Rob said.

I answered, "Only if he can take a solo in every song, that's the deal"

Their faces twisted and they responded with "What, is he crazy?"

"You already know the answer to that one; besides, he was only kidding." I told them to bring their gear into the house that we were rehearsing in the drum room and everyone broke into a smile.

Dave blurted, "Air conditioning!" As soon as we entered, Dad stopped playing.

"Sounded great," Jeff said; the rest of the guys nodded in agreement. I knew this was going to be an exciting evening; it seemed like it took forever for everyone to set up the equipment and get their axes in tune. Finally the moment arrived, and we were ready.

"How 'bout a jam in C?" asked Jeff,

Dad set the tempo, "One, two, three, four," laid down a driving beat and off we went. That first jam with live drums was an amazing experience also; I didn't think five people playing together with a new musician could sound so good. After about twenty minutes, the jam came to an end with a colossal garage ending. A garage ending is when everyone in the band kind of solos together for some time, then with eye contact, everyone ends the song together with a tumultuous crash.

The first sound spoken was from guess who: "What, are you guys trying to kill me? I'm old, you know!" Everyone laughed as we all knew what dad meant; it was ecstatic! The jam was inspirational, driving, and above all, intensely musical; we knew from that point forward our original music was going to be just fine.

We started doing our original music the very next rehearsal,; sometimes dad wouldn't join us until we worked the chords and vocals, and then he'd help with the arrangements. He is very good with arranging. It took us about a year to get our repertoire together; we had enough material for a two-hour performance.

At the end of this one particular rehearsal, dad stated, "Well, guys, we've been rehearsing close to a year now; it's time to make a move. You've written some great songs and we've put together some outstanding arrangements; we should step out or we might start to lose our momentum. We don't want to get stale; we want to be fresh and intense."

After we packed up our gear, we all went into the family room to discuss our options.

Rob began, "Maybe we can get a few small gigs locally to get a feel of playing in a live situation. We think our music is good but we really haven't gotten any feedback from others except our family and friends."

"Do you think we should try to get an agent?" I said. My father almost flew out of his recliner.

"An agent, what, are you crazy? They're like bandits with a license! You have to be very careful if you do contact an agent; make sure, check his or her credentials and reputation before talking with them. In the past, my experience with talent agents has been shaky at best, and one was a very good friend. He went under the name of Joe Drift; believe me, there were times we drifted, all right, from one end of the country to the other; plus, some of the establishments we played were pretty shady."

"We wound up calling him 'Snow Drift,' because a lot of the places we played we went into totally blind; sometimes we had to alter our repertoire completely to fit the situation and that's not easy. Although I guess today it's quite possible you could find and check out an agent over the internet, I'm sure there are a lot more possibilities."

Dad always manages to wind up thinking positively and up to date, he passed on experience from his past without being stuck in that past.

Jeff spoke up, "From my experience it's always best to play in front of a live audience; perhaps we can find a hall or something where we can sell tickets and with that money at least recoup our expenses."

Dave said quietly, "What about the Civic Center on Jackson Street?" There was a silence that seemed to last several minutes; everyone seemed to be considering the possiblity.

Finally Rob began, "Everyone is used to events at the Civic Center; they have plays, music and lectures, and maybe we should check into what it would cost to rent it for a night."

"Don't forget that there will be other expenses, such as tickets and advertising," I said.

Dad added, "You would have to pay agent fees and travel money if we had to go out of town, plus the possibility of equipment rental; I believe with the Civic Center that would be all-inclusive. Say we are able to rent the Center a couple of months from now; that would give us inspiration, plus we could start collecting dues that we would use to pay for the extra expenses such as advertising. I think Von's mom and I could help with that part. However, you are going want to see how the Civic Center wants to get paid."

"I don't have to go into work until three in the afternoon Monday and I have no school. I'll stop at the Center and check out the situation," I said.

"I'll go with you; I can meet you there at ten in the morning," Rob added. It was getting late and there wasn't much more we could do, so we set up the next rehearsal, saying we would keep in touch until then.

Rob and I pulled into the Civic Center parking lot at almost the same time; it was a little before ten. We discussed what we would say and walked towards the front entrance. When we got there, a sign was taped on one of the doors: "Please use the side entrance and ring the bell." An arrow was pointing to the left side of the building.

Anxiously we walked around to the left and located the door; Rob rang the bell, no answer. Rob rang it again, pushing even harder as if that would make the bell sound louder. After what seemed like an eternity, an attractive middle-aged woman opened the door.

"Hello, are you the fellas coming to clean and wax the stage floor?"

"No, ma'am, we're here to see about renting the Center for an evening," Rob replied.

"Come on inside," she said. We followed her through a hallway, then a door that let us through the back stage to another door which was her office.

"Please sit down; grab those chairs by the wall and come over to the desk. My name is Tina; I manage the center. What can I do for you?" What luck—the manager of the center! I spoke first.

"Hi, Tina, I'm Von and this is Rob." Rob nodded and said hello. I continued, "Well, Tina, we have a band, we play original music, and we'd like to have a concert here. Is that possible?"

"I don't see why not; what is the name of your band and what style of music do you play?" Rob and I just looked at each other; we'd forgotten to name the band!

Both of us were stammering sheepishly when Rob blurted, "*Olderyoung!*"

I knew what he meant and thought to myself, "Not too shabby."

"That's an unusual name; what about your musical style?" Tina said.

"I would say our music is based on the hard rock

from the sixties and seventies with a modern original twist. It is hard to describe; we're rehearsing this evening. Would you like to come hear us for yourself, say about seven o'clock?" I answered.

"Sure, I'll be there" responded Tina. Next came the hard part.

Rob began, "Supposing you like what you hear; what does the rental involve and what it will cost us, and how do we pay?"

"Before I give you boys the details, let me hear your band; then we can work things out," Tina replied. With that, we said our goodbyes; we told Tina we could find our way to the door and began to leave. When we got to the back stage area, we walked up to the curtain, pulled it back slightly, and stood there for a minute and imagined what it would be like to be on that stage playing before a full house.

Finally we were outside at our cars in the parking lot; we'd been silent until then. I spoke first.

"*Olderyoung*—how in the world did you come up with that on the spot?"

"I didn't," said Rob, "I'd actually been thinking about that name for some time, you know, with your dad being the drummer." About then we both realized we were so excited we could jump out of our shoes.

"I'll tell dad and call Jeff; you tell Dave, OK?" I said.

"No problem, see you tonight!" Rob replied as he unlocked his car and sat himself behind the wheel.

I was so excited I knew it was going to feel like a year until this evening got here.

The evening finally did come and you could feel the excitement and energy in the drum room. Not much was said as we tuned up and prepared for Tina to show up. Dad spoke first.

"Guys, I think tonight before Tina gets here, we should jam to get loose; we've been playing these songs for over a year, and we'll play a couple of our best we she gets here. In the meantime, these first few minutes should be for us." Everyone figured Dad was the experienced musician, so why not? We all agreed, picked a key to play in, Dad counted of the tempo, and off we went.

After a few minutes, the butterflies and jitters were gone as they'd been expelled by the "smokin' jam." We finished our jam; it was still a little before seven, so Rob and Dave went outside for a smoke. The rest of us went to the kitchen to get something to drink. When Rob and Dave returned, they had someone else with them: it was Tina. Rob had already introduced Dave to Tina so I proceeded to introduce the rest of the band.

"Hi Tina, this is Jeff; he plays keyboards. And this is my dad, Ennis—he plays the drums."

"Hi, it's nice to meet you all," said Tina, "*Olderyoung*. I get it!" Dad, Dave, and Jeff seemed surprised, as in the excitement, we forgot to tell them about the naming-of-the-band episode. We offered Tina a seat and gave her a set of ear plugs, as the sound could get pretty loud in the rather small room.

We picked the three songs we wanted to play for her, dad clicked the tempo with his sticks, and we began to play. We went right from one tune to the next just like we were playing a mini set; in all the three songs took close to twenty minutes. The last song we played consisted of a garage ending so it took several seconds for the musical din to die down. All eyes and ears were on Tina as she removed her earplugs; we also removed our headsets, for the time of reckoning had come.

She had a huge smile on her face. "Guys that was great, a wonderful original sound! Do you think the drummer can make it through the whole concert?"

Dad, never one to mince words said, "Just try me, lady!" We all laughed; I asked Tina if she would like something to drink.

"Iced green tea would be fine if you have some." Dad drinks that stuff all the time.

"I'll get it for you," he said.

We all moved to the family room to discuss the details of renting the Civic Center; I introduced my mom, who was sitting working on her laptop.

"This is my mom, Glenda."

"Pleased to meet you," Tina responded.

My mom offered to shake her hand and answered, "Likewise." In the next hour, Tina laid out all the details of renting the center; everything seemed feasible. However, we would have to come up with a five hundred dollar deposit before a date could be set. Mom said that wouldn't be a problem and wrote the five hundred dollar check on the spot.

Tina also said if the remaining sum of money needed to rent the center was not met by ticket sales, we would have to come up with the rest within thirty days. That was the only scary part; we knew we had our work cut out for us selling enough tickets to pay the remaining rent of twenty-five hundred dollars. Tina also said we would only have to bring our instruments and microphones; a sound system and sound engineer would be provided. A date was set for six weeks from Saturday; it was risky but we all wanted to give it a try.

We started advertising the next time the Tullahoma News was published. We decided on a four-by-five block ad worded in a way as to whet the interest of music fans of all types and ages.

"Do you like rock n' roll, jazz, heavy metal, original music from local musicians that will have you dancing in the aisles? Guaranteed or your ticket price refunded! Original Music by Olderyoung! We dare you not to come to this indoor happening! The Civic Center, Saturday, August 5th." Tickets *available on line at tullahomaciviccenter@ computercafe.com or at local participating stores, also in person at the Civic Center. Tickets will be available at the door the night of the concert."*

No picture accompanied the ad, just bold stand-out lettering in an outlined box. The ad would cost us fifty dollars a week; we had enough money from our dues to handle the cost. Tina said she would supply the tickets as part of the Civic Center package.

We rehearsed with a passion for those next six weeks, not learning anything new, but honing the songs we had already written. In a way, those weeks flew by, but at the same time seemed to take forever. Ticket sales were fair to middling according to Tina; about a week before the concert, we were still about one thousand dollars shy of the rent.

Finally, the day of the concert arrived; we had packed all of our equipment the night before. Dad took a vacation day so he could help us get everything together. I don't think any of us slept more than five minutes that night. We had all of our equipment in and set up on the stage before one in the afternoon; the sound engineer would not show up until five. What's the matter with that guy, what if something goes wrong?

Five o'clock finally arrived, the sound engineer (Dan was his name) cranked up the sound system, and we were ready for the sound check. As I looked out from behind the curtain, I noticed people beginning to mill around; time was getting near for the big moment. Dan suggested we play a jam; he said that would give him time to make adjustments and it might help us get loose—he sounded like someone else I know.

Before a note was played, however, we all tuned our instruments and Dad his drums. The sound was really different as it belted out of the huge sound system; finally, with everyone in tune, Jeff said, "Let's go with good ol' G." We nodded; Dad counted off and away we went!

We were still behind the curtains so we were

pretty relaxed, although they were opened just enough so we could see Dan at the mixing board. Dan was satisfied with the sound, as were we, so the jam came to close. As we finished, a splash of applause came from the early birds in the audience; all of our faces lit up with pleasure.

"Don't get big heads!" said Dad; six o'clock, one hour to go.

At a quarter to seven, from behind the curtain we could hear a rumbling in the audience; I peeked out from behind the curtain and I almost swallowed my tongue; a full house! The other guys peeked out too; I'll never forget. I can see it as if it were yesterday.

Dave, the bass player, started saying he couldn't feel the strings and he thought his fingernails were sweating. Jeff, our usually cool keyboardist, said his keys were all running together; they looked like an ice cream sandwich. Dad kept quietly tapping on his drums as if they would never make the proper sound and I think he was mumbling obscenities that would best be held to sailors at sea. Rob asked if anyone knew how to play guitar because he'd forgotten how. For me, if my legs were any wobblier, I could have called myself Jell-o Man; guitar picks kept squirting out of my fingers.

Just then Tina walked back stage. "You guys ready to rock and roll? I'm about ready to announce you to a sold out crowd, congratulations!"

She walked through the curtain to one of the microphones. Rob whispered, "Help me."

Dad came out from behind the drums. "OK,

guys, what's going on here? First, I want to say it has been an honor and a pleasure working with you. You have to remember I'm basically a jazz musician and I've spent the last fourteen months rehearsing with you guys because I think you are very good; you have all the traits to be great musicians if you apply yourselves. Those people out there paid their hard-earned money to see us perform and we're not going to let them down."

"Every time I played music, I got butterflies and the jitters; tuning my drums is an outlet, but when the curtain opens, I'm going to play my best for every note of every song. So come on, guys this, is nothing more than the drum room with people. I know you can go out there and play your butts off! Oh, and one last thing—is Dave in?"

"Yeah guys we can blow them away!" I chirped. Suddenly calm came over everyone; Dave stood up grasping firmly on his bass, Jeff looked down at his keys with the confidence of an experienced pro, and Rob looked over at us and said, "Let's play!"

We heard Tina's voice next. "Thank you all for coming here tonight! I'm Tina Sutherland, coordinator of the Civic Center. Tonight, you are about to embark on a journey of original music that will enlighten you whether you are young or old. So get ready to tap your toes and move to the beat. Please give a warm welcome to *Olderyoung*!" The stage curtains opened; one, two, three, four! That's how it all started.

The Legend & Adventures of Mechanico Man #2:
The Arrival of Professor Cosmoko & His Laws of the Universe

It has been several weeks since our friend Tim Boatman has changed to his alter ego Mechanico Man, nor has he heard from Sarsun and the Council of Planets. Tim, Zip, and their wives have settled into a 'normal' routine; this is about to change.

Chapter #1

Summer had given way to the beginning of fall. Tim watched in amazement as his wife Abigail transformed her multicolored summer gardens into the vibrant red and gold shades of autumn. Her summer toils were now expressed in red, green, yellow and gold peppers, marigolds, and chrysanthemums. Along with the harvesting, canning, and freezing of Abby's produce and herbs from the summer, they would be set for the usually mild Tennessee winters. As for Tim, he started to tinker with, you guessed it, speedboats! He knew better than to get carried away this time, and treated it strictly as a hobby.

The amazing laptop computer that Sarsun and the Council of Planets left for Zip's use allowed him to access massive amounts of scientific information. This information came from all parts of the universe. Satellites, alien planetary transmissions, and other sources, even our own satellites and telescopes floating in space provided countless megabytes of information. Zip realized how much Sarsun and the Council trusted Mechanico Man and himself. Zip ingeniously used some of the more commonly known and accepted theories to start a web site offering bits of information on his site through a weekly newsletter called "OOTWR" (pronounced "ootwar"), "Out Of This World Reality." Subscribers signed up for a newsletter, plus there was a blog for subscribers to respond and discuss the newsletter's sometime controversial topics.

Zip's wife Crystal was pretty much resigned to taking care of most of the household responsibilities, as prying Zip away from his computer for meals and sleep was about all she could expect. Yep, things were pretty normal for the two families; however, they all knew the situation could change at a phone call's notice.

Tim and Abby were sitting by the lake one evening when Tim's special cell phone began to vibrate. He looked at Abby, then answered.

"Hello, Sarsun?"

"Hello, Tim; I hope you are well and at peace."

"I'm fine, Sarsun, how 'bout you?"

"Personally, I am well, Tim." Sarsun's voice quickly became serious. "As you know I only contact you when we need the services of you and your friend. Transform yourself to Mechanico Man and I will contact you and Zippo in one hour."

Tim closed the phone, "You know what this means, Abby; I'm on another mission. Sarsun will contact Zip and me in about an hour." Abby and Tim walked arm in arm back to the house to await his assignment.

Abby had never seen her husband transform into Mechanico Man; she couldn't imagine him transforming into a proportionate being eight feet tall. When the time came for him to transform; Abby asked, "Tim, could you do what you do to become your alter ego so I can watch?"

Tim was slightly hesitant to answer. "Abby I don't know what happens myself; the transition is instantaneous. Sure, just to be safe, you'd better put on your sunglasses and watch from the doorway in the hall in case of something unexpected." They kissed; then Abby walked into the hallway.

Tim tapped the blank cell phone button twice; and before you could say twice he was Mechanico Man! Tim looked at Abby; her face had this astounded, surprised look. Before her was this large-looking figure in a shimmering metallic-looking uniform that just seconds ago was her loving husband.

"Abby, you O.K.? This is still me in here."

Finally able to speak, she replied, "Tim, even your voice is different; it's much deeper. I didn't see anything; one second, you're Tim, and the next this, this, hulk! You're my kinda man, Tim Boatman."

"Excuse me, ma'am, the name is Mechanico Man; all my friends call me "Mech." They both enjoyed a good laugh, any tension between them relieved. Tim knew no matter what form Abby saw him in, she would be forever by his side.

"Is it warm in that outfit?"

"The suit is completely temperature-controlled and has many amazing, almost unbelievable functions. Check this out, Abby." Mech was cut short as his Zune and headphones sprang to life. "This will have to continue later, Abby, I gotta go!"

He reached out, touched her hand, and then in an instant was gone. The room now empty, Abby could feel a smile on her face, realizing Tim's touch was warm even through that crazy suit.

Chapter#2

Just before transforming, out of habit he called his friend Zip to let him know they were on another assignment. However, this was hardly necessary, as Zip was notified the same time as Tim. Tim did it as it added a personal touch to his relationship with his old friend.

The first words he heard from Zip when he reached this strange looking destination were "Mech, you're not in Kansas anymore!" Zip was paraphrasing a line from "the Wizard of Oz." Before Mech could respond, Zip's laptop screen lit up with the image of Sarsun.

Mech reached for his Zune; however, it didn't feel the same. Pulling it out of his pocket, he realized his Zune and phone had become one. The object was about the same size as his Zune, only now phone buttons were located on the back side. The buttons were protected with a special protective coating. By now, Sarsun's image was on his new device's screen.

"Greetings; I hope you are both well and at peace. Mechanico Man, we've combined your phone and Zune together. We felt this would be more convenient; it is called a Zhone."

Knowing Mechanico Man would figure out the device, he continued. "I've brought you to the rings of Saturn. This is the safest place in our universe to transmit information without the chance of being detected. Gentlemen, we have ourselves a new and multifaceted problem that the Council nor I ever expected the likes of: our adversary, the legendary Professor Cosmoko! He has been known to refer to himself as a *Devotee of the Cosmos.* We have heard of him, but only as a legend; no one had ever seen the actual person."

"Basically the legend says Professor Cosmoko is from another dimensional universe bent on changing our universe. The legend says he's done this to several others. Legend also says that his universe is five billion light years away! With that astronomical figure, we left it at that, legend. However, we have now received a transmission from one of our patrol ships just outside of our universe that he's been spotted, or at least that's what we think. According to legend, when this incident took place, he was building a time machine that would enable travel to anywhere he desired. It still doesn't seem possible, but just in case, Mech, we want you to check out the situation."

"Once he enters our universe, there is a star in the Taurus cluster; we want you to engage him there. Let's see if he really is Professor Cosmoko. Mech, in this particular case, you can keep in touch with me; push the number one button on your Zhone and it will open a secure telepathic channel. I'm sure eventually you'll be able to reach me at will. This is the only way any of us communicate from this point, through telepathy. Best of luck, Sarsun out."

Mech and Zip would have to adjust their thinking again, so to speak; every thought, public or private, is transmitted to the other. Trust, honor, and respect are essential and as best as possible, undesirable thoughts should be blocked. Sarsun told them the last time they worked together it would become a natural process the more they used telepathy, even between the three of them. The coordinates were downloaded in both of their devices with Mechanico Man's again being processed right into his psyche.

"Here we go, Zip!" Mech thought.

"I'm right with ya, buddy; let's get this show on the road!" Once again, Mechanico Man had the sensation of floating, even though he was traveling faster than the speed of light.

"Hey, Mech, on my laptop screen you have that look you had when you were invisible." The suit had changed Mech to invisible while he was traveling to his destination. "I don't know who this guy is but the council is sure being cautious." Zip was correct in surmising the importance of taking all precaution against the legendary Cosmoko.

Tim sensed that he might be on a small asteroid. "That you are, my friend; the asteroid is no more than fifteen meters across and it seems to be circling around a small moon," responded Zip. Telepathy was a great advantage over speaking; it was extremely efficient.

The asteroid seemed to be keeping in exact rotation with the moon's night side, or was it? As the asteroid approached daylight, its orbit reversed, sending it back into darkness. Very unusual, the asteroid was always in perpetual night orbit or half orbit to be accurate. This solar system, if that's what you'd call it, had three weak suns.

A star map appeared showing Mechanico Man his location in reference to Professor Cosmoko, who was near the Taurus cluster; it also showed the solar system and the crazy half orbit of the asteroid. Revolving around these three suns was a ragtag conglomeration of planets, moons and asteroids. The boys could see why this location was chosen, basically a throw-away solar system with no resources, and not much exploratory value other than scientific. Besides, nothing scientists on Earth launched had come this far out anyway.

They didn't have much time to dwell on the matter as a strange image appeared on their screens. Flying in a craft that looked like it belonged in a Buck Rogers movie was this being that for all intents and purposes looked like a comical mischievous character from the same type of movie.

Professor Cosmoko's Time Machine

The supposed time machine looked like a rocket designed by H. G. Wells with a windshield and dash board that looked like they were taken out of a ninety-fifty Cadillac convertible. Hot Rod flames ran down the side of the craft. On either side were two glowing green panels; they seemed to be an energy source. Zip would confirm this was true.

As for the Professor himself, "who woulda thunk it," which is what Mech and Zip were doing. He looked almost oriental with long straight brownish colored hair tied back into a ponytail with two ends. His complexion was a greenish tint with yellow highlights; his thin lips were crimson red. His jaw was very square, almost artificial looking; the same went for his eyebrows. They were straight and moved almost mechanically. You could not see his eyes as they were behind what looked like sunglasses; however, they were not attached across the nose and you could not see through the lenses.

He seemed to be wearing flowing robes as if he were royalty. Neither transmitted any thoughts for several seconds; they seemed to be stunned, and finally Mech thought, "This is the threat to our universe?"

Chapter #3

"How are we seeing him like that? He's traveling at amazing speed, yet we see him as if he's riding down the interstate." Suddenly Zip got his answer.

"It seems he's in a vortex where it appears as if he's just cruising along."

"I guess I'm going to have to penetrate the vortex, Zip." Before Mechanico Man had a chance to implement the process of entering the vortex, Sarsun came into their thoughts.

"Greetings; I feel I must warn you. Do not let the comical look of Cosmoko deceive you; it is said he is ruthless and will annihilate anyone who poses even the smallest threat to him or his mission. If he thinks you can be of some use to him, even for entertainment, he will spare you. Your idea of entering the vortex is a good one, Mech, and you are not vulnerable to any of his tactics, but we don't want him to know that."

"As you try to enter the vortex, a shield will go up, preventing anyone from entering without Cosmoko knowing. We could get by the shield; however, as you try to enter, Mech, he will receive a warning; this will be in aid of keeping your abilities a secret. Once he sees you on his view screen, which is in the windshield, out of curiosity, let's hope he will let you enter the vortex."

"I actually believe he is expecting you; it will be up to you to gain his confidence. Zip will be able to monitor if anything unusual is going on while you are with him. Have full faith in your suit, Mech, and don't worry; information will be provided to both of you if needed. Are there any questions?" Neither Mech nor Zip answered.

"Very well, then, best of luck; Sarsun out."

Mechanico Man took a deep breath and headed towards Cosmoko's time machine. Again Mechanico Man felt the floating sensation and immediately arrived just outside of detection of the craft's shield.

Zip told Mech, "The best angle to be detected without suspicion was from either side about 50 meters from the time machine."

"Roger that!" replied Mech. They had their first telepathic laugh.

"Be careful friend."

Mechanico Man no sooner arrived along side Cosmoko's time machine when he heard, "Well, hello!" Mechanico Man was inside the vortex.

The vortex was something Mechanico Man had never seen or imagined. It felt warm and breezy like the kind of day at the lake his alter ego Tim Boatman loved so much. Instead of being dark and starlit like the rest of outer space, it had the appearance of dawn or dusk, very pleasant; not something you'd expect of someone with a reputation like Professor Cosmoko.

"I've been expecting you. I thought perhaps beings from your universe would try to intercept me, but I never thought they would send a messenger. That sure is a strange outfit you're wearing—seems you would need more than that in the void of space. How did you get here anyway? I detected no type of space craft in the area. Oh, and excuse me; allow me to introduce myself. I'm Professor T. Cosmoko, devotee of the cosmos, ruler of the three adjoining universes and soon the whole cosmos. Please come sit in my time vehicle I call CEPS, short for Continual Energy Propulsion System." Mechanico Man was just outside the vehicle, moving at the same speed as Cosmoko, although not under his own power.

Mechanico Man's head was spinning, so much happening in what seemed like a few seconds; he had to gather his thoughts. He wasn't quite sure but he thought Cosmoko was actually speaking.

"Yes, he is speaking," Zip passed on to him. On top of everything else, Cosmoko's time vehicle expanded to seat Mechanico Man along side him. He obliged Cosmoko and took the seat inside the time vehicle.

The inside of the vehicle looked impishly simple; in fact, it did look like the dashboard of a ninety-fifty Cadillac! Just as Sarsun predicted, a message flashed into Mech's head.

"Your name to Cosmoko will be Captain Vic Crown; you are a member of the Universal Space Patrol."

Again Cosmoko asked," and you are?"

"My name is Vic Crown I'm a captain in the Universal Space Patrol from the Council of Planets. I was dropped off close by; the council felt in this way we could show our intensions aren't hostile."

"I don't know," countered Cosmoko, "in your universe there is a solar system where the third planet from the sun has inhabitants, entities if you will, that are hell-bent terrorists. I've seen transmissions where people will actually blow themselves up to kill off a few of their own species. They seem to think they will gain salvation. How do I know you're not one of those people?" It was at this point Mech realized how Cosmoko spoke perfect English.

"I'm sure your scanners and detection devices aboard this craft already told you that was not the case, you would not have let me in. How do I know you are real? You're supposed to be myth, a legend. How is it you speak perfect English; how do I know you are not a machine programmed and hell-bent on destroying part or all of our entire universe? How do we know this isn't the reason for your return?"

"I like your style, Captain; no beating around the bush, right to the point. Until you can somehow prove differently, I am real. I use the English language as it was the most prevalent in transmissions received from your universe. It would seem an empty, wasted venture if I came to destroy your universe, although that possibility is not out of the question. I'm hoping the important leaders of your universe are civilized enough to want to sit down and discuss the situation at hand."

"He's real, all right, Mech. I'm still working on trying to understand his time vehicle and its capabilities. Your suit is sending back information, another function to add to the list. I'll let you know stuff as soon as I do. Zip out."

"Would mind telling me what the situation at hand means, Professor?"

"Not so fast, Captain. I think it would be in you and your universe's best interest if you arrange a meeting between myself and your leaders. I will meet where ever they choose. Let me reiterate, I will not leave until I meet with your leaders. Here is a transmitter I will contact you with when you have assembled your leaders and arranged a proper meeting place." Cosmoko handed Mech a black and silver transmitter and waved. Before Mechanico Man could reply, he was outside the vortex in the exact location in space he had entered.

"Looks like he's an illusionist, too," thought Mechanico Man as he placed the transmitter into his uniform.

Chapter #4

"Greetings; I hope you are well. I'll forego the 'and at peace'—seems peaceful would be the last thing on you fellas' minds." Sarsun was the first to speak after Mech's meeting with the professor. "Zip, I hope you were able to gather as much information as possible while Mech was on the time vehicle. Mechanico Man, I want you to meet me here on Auroari. As you arrive, change back to Tim Boatman; you will go to these co-ordinates and I will meet you there. What we did with you when you were here previously is top secret, even on our planet. No one knows of your alter ego. It does not matter how peaceful a planet is; you must always be on the lookout for spies who sometimes disguise themselves as our own citizens."

"I'm working on the information, Sarsun; there are all kinds of data to decipher but it's not easy." Zip finally entered the conversation.

"Good, Zip, I know you'll do your best; see you soon, Mech, Sarsun out."

"Wow, Mech, you get to go to Auroari and meet the leader of the Council of Planets, you lucky dog you! I guess in this particular instance I envy you. I sure didn't envy you when you were about to be exploded to pieces in that fuel plant."

"You know what, Zip? I'm actually a little nervous. Sarsun seems like a respected, tolerant, and powerful leader. I wonder how far you can push that tolerance. Well, I'm at the co-ordinates; next time you see me I'll be plain ol' Tim Boatman."

In an instant, Mechanico Man was again Tim Boatman. He arrived out of nowhere into the Capitol City of Evols. His appearance in the square at midday didn't seem to faze anyone; it was if it happened all the time. In his pockets were the Zhone and Cosmoko's transmitter.

"It's amazing, Zip; I'm not wearing the same clothes I left home with. I'm dressed like the natives of this planet. Cool material; it's as if I don't have anything on. I've never experienced anything like this."

"That was probably one of the most amazing things I've seen so far Mech, I mean Tim, I mean Captain. First an aerial image of the Capitol City with the city's name across the bottom appeared, then the city square. I no sooner focused my eyes to the surroundings when *phoof,* you appeared out of nowhere! But that's not all; here is a city full of citizens going about their business as usual when you arrive. By the way Tim, the first four letters of the city's name in reverse spell *love;* add on the s, and you've got loves."

The Capitol City of Evols was a perfect example of humankind working with their planet. Every imaginable environmental technology and concept was being used thorough out the city. The use of solar energy and wind power was incorporated where ever practical. Every building also had a power supply that looked like it was right out of the Nikolas Tesla's blueprints. The air was fresh, clean, and easy to breathe. Tim assumed this was because there might be a bit more oxygen in their atmosphere.

The city itself was as fresh and clean as the air. The architectural design flattered the surrounding landscape, creating a vision of flawless beauty. Tim felt completely secure and at ease in the capitol city of Evols on the planet Auroari.

"From my laptop, Tim, I was able to look at a complete overview of this planet; it is truly astonishing, especially how advanced their technology is over ours here on Earth. I also know Auroari is the fourth planet from its twin suns; there are a total of seven planets in this very small but unusual solar system. Five of the seven planets actually support some form of life. These five planets revolve almost side-by-side in a synchronous orbit around their suns. Our satellites and probes have not come anywhere near this part of the universe. "

Before Zip could utter another word, Sarsun appeared on his computer screen. Almost simultaneously at Tim's side was the man himself, Sarsun, leader of the Council of Planets!

"Zip and I knew with you there wouldn't be much time for sightseeing." Tim was again speaking aloud. Sarsun and Tim laughed, shook hands, and exchanged a friendly embrace. Sarsun was considerably taller than Tim; he had the build of a seasoned warrior, although his demeanor was very relaxed and easy-going. Tim looked upon Sarsun with great respect and gratitude.

"Greetings; I hope you are both well and at peace. Excellent, Zip, I see you have already learned many things about our planet and solar system. This shows me you have the makings of— what do they call it on Earth? Oh yes, the makings of sleuth. Tim, it is great to see you in person again." Tim looked puzzled.

"Remember, Tim, I saw you when we first reassembled you. Let's you and I go somewhere to sit, chat, and take of some refreshment. I know just the place; we can walk to it from here." Tim liked the idea; after all how many earthlings get the leader of the Council of Planets to take them for some refreshment. For that matter, how many earthlings knew of Sarsun!

After walking several minutes, they came to a small café overlooking a beautiful park with walkways and fountains. During their walk, Tim remained silent, taking in all of the advancements in building and street design and traffic flow; there was hardly any. What vehicles he did see hovered about six inches above the road and were completely silent, just about the same as the vehicles the Grays used on their planet, he thought.

"Come, Tim; they have a table waiting for us overlooking the park." Sarsun led them up a few steps to a balcony with a view of the park. There was a small table by the railing; a waiter was ready for them.

"Hello, sir, please be seated. What can I get for you and your guest?"

"I'll have my usual, Fayelon, and give the Captain the same. Fayelon, this is Captain Vic Crown of the Universal Space Patrol. Don't worry, Captain, you'll enjoy the beverage, I'm sure." Fayelon left to get their drinks.

"Can I order you something to eat; shall I call Fayelon back?"

"No thank you, Sarsun, I have too many butterflies to eat right now."

"Butterflies—that is an insect on your planet. I see no butterflies."

"It's an expression, Sarsun; it means I'm a little nervous."

"Well, Tim, there are a few things I have to tell you; I hope they won't give you more 'butterflies.'"

"I know to Professor Cosmoko, you are Captain Vic Crown, and now here on Auroari, you are Representative Captain Vic Crown of the Universal Space Patrol. As I told you before, we must keep the utmost secrecy about you from everyone; you are unique, Tim. From this point on, I will address you here as Captain Vic Crown. Also, Tim, before you look in the mirror, I must advise you do not look exactly like the Tim you know. We've added some facial hair so your personal life won't be compromised just in case. As I said before, you can never be to careful, especially in this situation. Oh, yes, don't be shocked, we thought you'd look distinguished with that hair color."

Tim could hear Zip laughing; even Sarsun smiled. How was he hearing Zip? He didn't have his uniform on, nor did he push any buttons on his Zhone. He glanced over at Sarsun, who also knew what he was thinking. Sarsun looked back and just shrugged his shoulders.

"I told you telepathy would come to you." Tim observed Sarsun wasn't speaking when he heard the response.

Everyone's attention returned to situation at hand. Sarsun leaned on the table and spoke to Tim.

"Research into the legend shows that Professor Cosmoko has a special interest in your planet. We felt rather than using your politicians, who are usually biased about something or other, you'd be a much better choice due to the fact you're kind of the representative for all living entities in this universe."

"I never thought of myself in that way, Sarsun; I'm basically a simple person."

Sarsun interrupted. "Tim, you are a highly intelligent being, and as for the simple part, all the better. The council feels your mentality is necessary for this meeting with Cosmoko. I've prepared quarters for you at my home, and you will be my guest; I insist. This is not unusual in these types of matters."

"Sarsun, I'm honored. Thank you; I hope I won't be any inconvenience."

"Not at all, and if you are finished with your beverage, we should be on our way. By the way, did you enjoy your drink? It is called *Shanar*. The word is from our ancient language, as are most of the names we use; the interpretation is *drink of many fruits*."

Tim thought, "That was a short visit," then answered, "Yes, it was very delicious, refreshing; thank you. I look forward to the opportunity to try it again."

"You're right; this was a short visit, but we have much to do. We shall visit the café another time. Let us go; I have a vehicle waiting." Tim saw was a slight smile on Sarsun's face.

Sarsun's vehicle was just through the park, about one half meter's walk from the café. The city had special areas allotted for vehicle parking;

otherwise no vehicle other than those traveling about were on any street.

What a vehicle! It was much different from the professor's antique-looking craft. It was the color of platinum, soft and pleasing to the eyes. As they approached within a few feet of the vehicle, doors opened from the seamless-looking exterior, again very similar to the vehicles in Rahufoya, only much more sophisticated.

Once inside, Tim observed that the interior was magnificent, plush yet simplistic. There was a small panel with a few pastel lights; the rest of the interior was built for comfort.

Once they were strapped in and seated, Sarsun spoke. "To my residence please, speed 85 *canto spheres.*" Without a sound, the vehicle propelled itself softly forward.

"Wow, Sarsun, you guys really are advanced! The vehicle goes wherever you tell it to; is it robotic? Is this interior changing color?"

"No Tim it is not a robot. We use an advanced system similar to your GPS system on Earth. The entire planet is divided into grids; each grid is monitored by a satellite. Once the voice command is given, a route is chosen unique to anyone else's, and you are safely transported to your destination at whatever speed you desire. As for the interior, the color does change according the outdoor surroundings, offering the passenger as pleasant and authentic view of whatever one might encounter in his or her travels."

After a breath-taking ride that seemed like only

a few moments, they arrived at Sarsun's residence. Once again, Tim was taken aback by the beauty of design. Sarsun's home looked as if grew right into the environment, simple architectural lines blending in perfectly with their surroundings, and what surroundings they were. This was the first time Tim really took in the trees, plants and other types of vegetation. Everything was very similar to Earth's except every plant seemed to possess an exotic beauty unique to itself. Shades of color unimaginable on living vegetation—Tim couldn't take it in all at once.

"Don't worry, Bud; I'm downloading the stuff on to my hard drive and you'll be able to have a closer look when you're not so busy." It was his good friend Zip; he hadn't contacted him since the café.

"I couldn't look at scenery either; I've been trying to decipher the information I received from Cosmoko and his CEPS Vehicle. I'm not having much luck; contact you later."

"Come into my home, Tim; make yourself comfortable. Unfortunately, unlike you and Zip, I have no mate, so my home has only a man's touch. There is residence on the back part of the property where another family lives, Rhim and Keera; they are caretakers in my employ. They do a wonderful job, so I can devote myself to the Council and the residents of this planet and the universe. Come, let us take some nourishment; it's vegetarian, I hope you don't mind."

"Makes no difference to me; actually, now I'm pretty hungry. I feel very relaxed at your place. It is very beautiful, Sarsun, again, simple but eloquent. Everything looks in perfect place, the openness of each room, how they flow together to compose a beautiful setting. There's a lot we could learn from your society to use on our planet." They were seated in a very beautiful room with an open view of Sarsun's estate. Wherever Tim looked outside or at another beautiful room, peace and tranquility flowed. For the first time since the beginning of this assignment, he thought about the love of his life, Abigail.

"Abby would think she was in heaven," he said aloud.

"All in due time, my friend," responded Sarsun. "For now let us enjoy our meal."

After they finished one of the best meals Tim had ever eaten, Sarsun said, "Come, Tim, let us enjoy the evening on the back patio. There we can observe a beautiful panorama of our twin suns setting as daylight fades to dusk. There is an amazing view of our night sky once the suns are gone. When the time approaches, Tim, I will point to the direction of you solar system; it is not visible with the naked eye. In the meantime, my friend, you do have the transmitter with you, as Cosmoko can call at any moment. Once notified, we only have a couple of hours to get the council together; this is why we must talk."

"Yes, I have the transmitter, Sarsun; it sort of came along when I arrived here. What's the deal with this guy Cosmoko? He seems to anticipate our every move as if he has advanced information."

"I can answer that!" As if the sound came from out of nowhere Zip's voice was in their presence. "I even know why Professor or should I say, King or Lord Cosmoko has come to our universe."

For the first time, Tim observed a curious, puzzled and somewhat surprised look on Sarsun's face.

"Please tell us what you know every bit of information is extremely important," Sarsun replied.

"Wait a cotton pickin' minute! Before we go any further, is this some form of telepathy too?"

"How am I hearing Zip, I have no type of device activated," asked Tim.

Sarsun chuckled. "I'll say one thing about you Earthlings; you have to know how every 'cotton pickin" thing works. That is a good thing, as you say. Our electrical frequencies are so powerful and advanced that we can transmit sound to a specific location. All I have to do is program my personal system located at the home's main power array. The array is similar to your circuit breaker box at home, although a lot more complex. Please continue, Zip; you were saying we should call him 'King or Lord' Cosmoko?"

"You guys won't believe this! Whether or not there is any truth in the information I was able to decipher, Cosmoko does live in another dimension. but it's nothing like you'd expect. I downloaded this information from the computers on his CEPS. The other dimension Cosmoko lives in is not like anything in our reality; it is almost like a fantasy land. For lack of a better description, through the ages, a place similar to this has been called by many names, the final resting place when you leave this mortal world. His mission, according to your interpretation, is either to conquer or convert the entire cosmos to his way of existence. He's coming to meet with the council to give you his *Laws of the Universe!*"

Professor Cosmoko with his Laws of the Universe

"Within these laws are by-laws and other

requirements for every citizen of the universe. Apparently, if you don't comply, there are assorted penalties. I don't have a copy of the actual laws; I will send you a copy of what information I have right away, Sarsun. In the meantime, I'll keep working on this guy. He's got this facade; even though everything points to him being real, I'm still not convinced."

"Thank you once again, Zip; your information has been invaluable as always. I will look forward to receiving the report. Keep up the good work; I'll be waiting to hear from you."

"Great work, friend!" Tim added.

The suns had set; as Sarsun promised, the view was magnificent. Sarsun pointed in the direction of Earth's solar system. Observing the foreign looking star clusters and an amber tinted moon that looked like you could reach up and grab, Tim was speechless.

Using a very earth-like phrase, Sarsun nudged Tim. "What's the matter, cat got your tongue?"

Before Tim could answer, the transmitter Cosmoko had given Tim began to resonate with a beautiful sound. Tim opened the device and listened.

"Greetings, Captain Crown, I hope you are well and at peace. I believe that's what your illustrious leader Sarsun would say; I hope he's nearby as this message is for the both of you." Neither Tim nor Sarsun spoke as Cosmoko continued.

"I'm sure by now you have figured the purpose of my mission, which is what I wanted you to do. I do not want this to seem a threat or allegation against your universe, however; please call your council to meet at exactly 0900 tomorrow morning I will be more specific when I arrive."

"We will be ready at that time, Professor. Can you possibly give us a little more insight into your plan?" Sarsun asked.

"I'm afraid that is all I am at liberty to say; I will see you at the council meeting." With that, another beautiful sound played from the transmitter, fading into the silence of the evening. Zip was the first to speak.

"I couldn't find the frequency of that transmitter; it's like he's on his own impenetrable time line or something."

"He is quite mysterious; I will give him that. I guess there is not much more we can do this evening. I will notify the council secretary with the meeting time for tomorrow morning. Until then, Tim, or should I say Captain Crown, make yourself comfortable. If there is anything you need, just call for one of my dear caretakers; they will be happy to be of assistance. I will take my leave for now; Tim and Zip, you'd both better get some rest also. Tomorrow promises to be a very interesting day right from the start." Sarsun patted Tim on the shoulder and disappeared into the house.

Tim preferred to remain outside, enjoying the view of a night like one he had never witnessed.

"Well, Zip, this sure beats working a day job. I have to say, though, I still don't see this Cosmoko as a threat. I guess we should do as Sarsun says and get some rest, although I hardly feel like sleeping. Let Abby know I'm OK, will you, Zip? And if you need me, don't worry about the hour; contact me at any time."

"I'll take care of everything, Tim. I gotta say, though, I am a bit exhausted; good night."

Chapter #5

Tim awoke the next morning to a beautiful view of the twin suns rising outside his bedroom window. He showered, dressed, and hurried towards the door to observe a better view of this outstanding sight. Not surprisingly, Sarsun was already present when he arrived outside.

"Good morning, Tim; I see you are an early riser like myself. Try some of this; it is similar to your coffee on earth." Sarsun handed him a warm brimming cup of dark fragrant liquid. Tim took a long sip before speaking.

"Yes, I am generally an early riser; however, that wasn't difficult this morning, considering our current situation. This stuff is really good; what do you call this beverage?"

"This beverage is called *Katamalonifer,* for the sake of a better word, Tim, Auroarian coffee. The citizens call it *Kat* for short; did you have the opportunity to rest?"

"I believe I nodded off for a couple hours, Sarsun, but that is about the extent of my rest. What is the time?"

"It is only six-thirty; we still have a couple of

hours before the trip to the council building. Come, let us retire to my study where we can enjoy breakfast and discuss today's agenda, if there is really an agenda to discuss. I'm sure our man Zip is still probably asleep anyway, so there's not much else we can do."

"Wrong go! I'm right here at your service!" chimed Zip, "and I might add I've already had my breakfast!" The three of them enjoyed an early morning laugh; they were becoming quite a team.

Tim enjoyed his breakfast, and after asking what a couple of items were, decided just to enjoy the flavors and taste, as every name seemed to be harder to pronounce than the next.

"Sarsun, I notice when I'm plain ol' Tim, there's nothing spectacular about myself, no super intelligence, just me. Yet when I become Mechanico Man, my intelligence seems limitless." He was expecting agreement from Sarsun; what he heard really surprised him.

"Tim, I wish I could say that were true; you only react to situations as they are presented to you. When you are Tim, your desire is to be Tim, but if the situation should arise, you have everything Mechanico Man has at his disposal. It is possible today will reveal some of this quality, for although we will all be seeing you as Tim, or should I say Captain Vic Crown, you might be called to some Mechanico Man processes."

Tim sat quietly and seemed to be in deep thought as how to understand what he was just told.

Sarsun continued, "It's nothing that should

concern you, Tim; I'm sure that all you do in the guise of Mechanico Man will more than justify you just being plain ol' Tim. You do really need to separate those personalities in order to maintain a healthy outlook on life. I just wanted to prepare you for these rare situations where you'll be Tim but have access to Mechanico Man abilities. By the way, you two, during the council meeting, I may try to communicate with you telepathically. I may need additional information, especially from you, Zip. It's time to go, Tim; come, my vehicle is waiting outside the front door."

There, hovering just above the ground, was the beautiful platinum vehicle; this time the doors were already open. Once they were seated, the doors closed and Sarsun gave the directions: "Planetary Council Building, 80 *canto spheres*."

The vehicle softly glided forward. They were on their way to meet and hear the legendary Professor Cosmoko. Neither Tim nor Sarsun had that much to say on the ride, except for Tim again commenting on the smooth ride and beautiful country side. They were at the council building in a matter of minutes. The building seemed to be in a different part of the city, more towards the outskirts of the city limits.

"Wow, this place is protected by all sorts of force fields!" Zip broke in.

"As I said before, you can be at peace, but you can never be too precautious; as you Earth people say, 'Better safe than sorry.'"

"Here's another thing Earth people say: 'It's show time!'" exclaimed Tim.

The council building was another feat in architecture, beautifully designed to fit into the surroundings. It had the look of an ancient Roman senate building, flowing lines with gracious columns lining the front entrance. Upon one's entering, it opened into one sprawling room with seats lining the perimeter as you would see in an ancient senate. In front of these seats were a row of long tables more like desks with places for electronic devices or whatever you might need to take part in whatever was happening that particular day. There were pitchers of drinking water every few feet along these desks. Apparently the most important dignitaries were seated at these desks.

As they passed through the doorway, Sarsun leaned towards Tim.

"Looks like we've copied some of your ancient masters." Sarsun led Tim to his seat, right alongside his at one of the long tables. In the center of the room towards the back was a podium where the main speaker stood.

"It's almost nine o'clock, 0900; will he really show?" Tim wondered.

Suddenly, without warning, the beautiful sound Tim heard through the transmitter filled the great room; the now hundreds of people in the building became silent. As if out of nowhere, the legendary Professor Cosmoko appeared standing behind the podium.

With the beautiful sound still playing softly in the background, Cosmoko began to speak.

"Greetings to the leaders of this wonderful and magnificent universe; I am Professor T. Cosmoko. Most of you have known of me only as legend, but as you can see, I am more than a legend. I am here in your physical reality. I have come to offer you a great opportunity."

With that, a great hologram appeared, showing a place of spectacular beauty. Combined with the beautiful sounds, the entire congregation seemed to be awestruck, almost mesmerized, as if in a trance. Sarsun stood to speak; as he was rising, he could hear Zip in his head.

"I got nothing; I can't seem to figure out how he's creating the projection or the sound."

"Professor Cosmoko, it is indeed an honor to have you in our presence; however your legend does not reveal you as a forthright individual. Have we been misled or do you feel you can get more flies with honey as opposed to vinegar?"

"My dear Sarsun, I have been portrayed in many ways, in many universes. I would ask that you hear what I have to say before passing judgment." Sarsun nodded in agreement and again took his seat.

Before continuing, Cosmoko somehow faded both the sound and hologram. "I hoped my non-abrasive entrance would put your minds at ease. I have something to offer you for eternal peace; you will be relieved from all war, pestilence, and disease. Allow me to show you."

Again appeared another hologram; this time, it looked like an ancient scroll. The large words across the top read **The Laws of the Universe**. Under that appeared many numbered laws with subtitles and amendments, far too much for a person to take in one meeting.

Cosmoko continued, "I don't want to startle you and I realize this is far too much for you to absorb at this time; I will leave enough copies for all the leaders of this universe, and they are being downloaded on to your electronic devices as we speak. I will give you time to absorb this information and return at a later date to discuss conditions."

Now in a forceful, concerned tone, Sarsun again spoke. "Excuse me, Professor, but it sounds to me that we have an ultimatum. My planet has not warred in centuries, yet your proposal does not sound like one of peace, especially when one ends a statement with discussing conditions. We've heard of your conquering other universes. I know I speak for every planetary system present; we have no intention of being conquered." A loud cheer of approval echoed throughout the council building.

"I assure all of you that you will not be conquered, as your illustrious leader has stated; you will, however, be without my protection. At that point, I cannot guarantee the safety of your universe or its inhabitants."

This time Captain Vic Crown spoke. "Professor, Sir, this universe has survived for many millennia with no one's protection; why would we need it now?"

"Captain, we meet again, and once more I detect

an arrogance. You are from the planet Earth, correct? Are there not war, pestilence, and disease still present? How long do you think that can go on before you finally self-destruct? I offer an end to such conditions; it is just the matter of following a few rules."

"Professor, it has been our perception that learning on our own will make us a better people. Sometimes that comes at a very dear and high cost. No one likes that scenario, but it is part of a process that builds character. On Earth, we are always trying to improve our condition; we've made some horrendous mistakes, but we are learning. I've been privileged to visit this beautiful and peaceful planet Auroari; there are many ideas I can take back to earth to continue to help improve our condition."

"Yes, Captain, that is true, but there are situations that you can't control, such as a comet or asteroid crashing into your planet, destroying all you've worked for in an instant. I can prevent that from happening. So as you all can understand, it will be a give-and-take condition; again, you must follow a few rules."

"Professor, sometimes a comet or asteroid is what is needed to cleanse a condition that can't be rectified in any other way. Somehow or other, the survivors of these incidents manage to pick up and start over; it is part of the process of life."

"You are indeed an interesting species; I don't believe I've ever encountered anyone or thing like you, Captain. I'm sure you are a qualified representative of your planet. It seems all of the representatives of this universe concur with your thinking. That, however, changes nothing; I will leave you with these rules and return at another time. Don't try to follow me, as I will not be visible."

Before anyone could say anything, the beautiful sound again filled the room; the hologram with the laws disappeared, along with Professor Cosmoko.

As Sarsun approached the podium again, he heard Zip: "The rules have been downloaded to my computer and there's no trace of the professor."

"Ladies and gentlemen, it seems we've had a most amazing visit," Sarsun began. "We should not panic or react until further research is done into the illustrious Professor Cosmoko. Go back to your respective planets; we will study **The Laws of the Universe** and convene again to discuss our options. Before you leave, please have some Auroarian delights; there is a hearty meal and entertainment across the street in the *Theater of Art*. Please relax and have a safe journey home. I hope you are well and at peace. Thank you for your valuable time; I will be in contact with all of you in the coming weeks."

Tim and Sarsun sat quietly as all the delegates filed out of the council building and across the street to the theater to relax before heading back to their respective planets.

"Well, Tim, there is not much left for you here; it looks as if Cosmoko plays by his own rules. That in itself is kind of perplexing, for it seems at least for now we have no control over his coming and going.

Zip, have you come up with anything?" Sarsun was speaking aloud as the building was now empty his voice echoing slightly.

"During that entire meeting, I was trying to find a way to decipher or break his code; it was like he knew exactly what we were up to. He even knew Tim was from earth. I'll bet he even knows who he is. When the laws appeared on my computer, it was like nothing I've ever witnessed; they were just there in a file folder."

Sounding slightly alarmed Sarsun replied. "Zip, do not open that folder until we can come up with more information; we don't know what effect it will have on our systems. I'm going to give you an interplanetary connection so you can notify every other leader to take the same precaution; I will send it through Tim's Zhone. In my haste and distraction,I forgot to pass that possibility on to the other delegates." Tim handed him the Zhone and he proceeded to send Zip the connection.

"Come, Tim, let us forget about what happened today and enjoy ourselves with the rest of the delegates, after which we can send you home. I'm sure Abby is missing you."

"She sure is," Zip chimed in.

Tim smiled and headed across the street with Sarsun. "Let her know I'm fine; I'll be home soon."

To be continued...